SAM CHAPMAN SWUNG DOWN FROM THE BAY.

He poked his head into the shed and gritted his teeth upon seeing the dead form of a man sprawled below a workbench. He was reaching a hand around the butt of his revolver when from behind him the all-too-familiar sound of a rifle being levered gave him pause.

"Go for it, mister!"

"My mammy didn't raise any stupid kids," Sam said, glad he'd pocketed his marshal's badge.

"What's your name, tough guy?"

"Name's Chapman. Look, I ain't hunting up trouble."

"Trouble is what you found, Chapman. Now just ease that little six-gun out of your hand, and turn so's I can get a good look at you."

In turning, Sam let go of the reins and his bay shied away. Too late, he saw the rifle butt heading for his face. . . .

ROBERT KAMMEN
HIGH PLAINS WANDERERS

ZEBRA BOOKS
KENSINGTON PUBLISHING CORP.

ZEBRA BOOKS

are published by

Kensington Publishing Corp.
475 Park Avenue South
New York, NY 10016

First printing: March, 1990

Printed in the United States of America

For my daughter-in-law, Kay,
and granddaughter, Jaime Lynn.

ONE

All that Rocky Boy dreaded had come to pass.

The Ojibwa Chippewa had become as one with the tumbleweed sent hither and yon by summery winds knifing across the high plains. No longer could the Ojibwa return to their ancestral lands in Canada, even though Rocky Boy, their aging chief, had not let his warriors join the Meti in their rebellious uprising against the provincial government. Other tribes who had taken part in the rebellion, the Canadian Cree under Little Bear and the Blackfoot led by their powerful chief, Crowfoot, had been forced to split into small bunches to elude Canadian troops forcing them southward across the border into Montana. Rocky Boy's Ojibwa had taken a more westerly course to avoid trouble along the way.

"Fair?" That question fled silently from between Rocky Boy's thick and grim-set lips. They were Indians, and thus suspected of having killed and burned down villages as had the Cree and Blackfoot.

Fairness had nothing to do with this bitter issue, nor had justice or morality. This was something he could not explain to his people trailing behind him, as he hunkered on his war pony.

But part of the trouble, pondered Rocky Boy, was that Little Bear was a son of Big Bear who had married the sister of Rocky Boy. This fact was known to the Indian agent and other provincial officials. So in their minds this blood bond had united the Cree and Chippewa, in peace and in war. Most of Rocky Boy's bitterness was directed at the Meti, for he felt they had exploited the Indians.

"This French half-breed, Riel," he said, "used our blood brothers."

One of his braves, Iron, nodded in agreement.

"They will hang Riel."

"And others." Though he was only in his late thirties, gray threaded through Iron's braided hair. Iron had thickset shoulders, a cleft in the upper lip, compliments of a Blackfoot hunting knife, and a hawkish, glowering face set in worried lines. For more than two weeks they had kept on the move, tiring out both their horses and others forced to make this long march on foot.

Jutting to the south was Bear Paw Mountain, east of that the Little Rockies, and it seemed to Iron they had come no closer since breaking camp well before sunup. Yesterday an outrider had dashed in to tell of a small band of Cree being pursued by provincial soldiers. With an order from Rocky Boy, his Ojibwa were brought into a coulee. It was here that an older squaw succumbed to the harshness of their forced trek. Only the warrior Iron glanced back at the

8

gravesite as they left the coulee. Others would die, he felt, before they reached the land along the Milk River. Now Iron slapped at and missed a horsefly that had settled on the shoulder of his pinto; he said gutturally, "That would have been my supper."

Rocky Boy mused that Iron's fear, and that of the other Ojibwa, was for the buffalo. Later that day a stand of gnarled oaks told Rocky Boy they had crossed into territorial Montana and were coming onto the northern fringes of the high plains. This was the summer bed ground of the buffalo. By his reckonings, dusk should find them arriving at the historic Milk River crossing used by Canadian Chippewa-Cree. As the day wore on—dusty, simmering under a piercing sun—only an occasional antelope or coyote ghosting away told the Ojibwa game was not as plentiful as in other years.

"But the buffalo . . . where are they?"

Surely by now they should have spotted a few small herds, or even a lonely bull. Passing closer to the western bank of Lodge Creek, Rocky Boy drew up his war pony on the grassy bank and stared pensively at his watery image. He saw the face of a man saddled with the destiny of the Ojibwa Chippewa. It was a strong face, with bold features leathered by the years, and almond eyes filled with a sad wisdom. Four eagle feathers tied at the back of his long, braided hair marked his status as a chief. Rocky Boy wore a simple buckskin tunic; at his ample belt rested a Green River knife, his other weapon the Sharps resting in the doeskin sheath. His eyes went to the wavy reflection of a dead and twisted oak standing just upslope, and he thought, trembling, that many would perish in the months to come. Not at the hand of the provincial soldiers or the white men settled down here. On their ancestral lands game had been plentiful, deer and moose and bear, with the lakes yielding northerns and walleyes. These plains seemed barren now that the white men had come in boldly to plow up virgin prairie grass, and in so doing either killed or driven the antelope and deer farther west toward the mountains.

"Many will die of starvation," he murmured bitterly. "We have been cast adrift from our ancestral lands. We are wanderers, Iron, wanderers of the high plains."

It was with a despairing glimmer in his eyes that Rocky Boy wheeled his gelding around and looked at those he led. At last count the Ojibwa had numbered just over a hundred: men, women, children. There were the subchiefs Iron, Washita, and the rebellious Coyote Walker. Part of the reason they had been forced off their ancestral lands was that Coyote Walker and a few followers had been there when a Cree war party had attacked the settlement at Ruby River. A foolish and damning act by the arrogant Coyote Walker. Further troubling Rocky Boy was Coyote Walker's bold statement that he should become chief of the Ojibwa.

"Killing is all that interests Coyote Walker!"

Startled by the angry words of Rocky Boy, the gelding fought the reins as it pranced sideways and snorted nervously through its nostrils. A quieter word from its rider brought the horse into an easy walk over prairie grass. As for Coyote Walker, mused the chief of the Ojibwa Chippewa, there must be an understanding between us. The warring days are over. Those who fought in that glorious battle at the Little Big Horn had been forced onto reservations, while a network of army posts had been strung across the vast reaches of northern Montana to protect white settlers from those Indians who had fled into Canada. Close at hand was the Fort Assinniboine military reservation, and once word got out that the Ojibwa were up along the Milk River, Rocky Boy expected a visit from an army patrol. He would tell these soldiers the Ojibwa had come down to live in peace.

"But—Coyote Walker—for him there shall never be peace."

A low rumble of thunder snatched Rocky Boy's words away, but not the Ojibwa Chippewa's bitter mood. He let a picture form in his mind of the timbered land far to the north, of marshy reaches and crystal-clear lakes, and of a vast blue sky stretching up to tundra land and beyond. Never again, he knew with a fatalistic certainty, would he see a place his bones ached to go back to again. Finally, around a rueful grimace, he said, "Let it go. For I must be strong . . . though I know my people grieve as I do for what we have lost. So let it go."

Again came the distant clamor of thunder, and Rocky Boy twisted to gaze off to the southwest. The clouds that had been building since first light dropped rain out of their black bottoms just as the Ojibwa caught their first glimpse of the Milk River. Swiftly the low storm front swept overhead, pouring out heavy, wind-driven rain, cooling to the touch,

11

though Rocky Boy knew it would hinder their progress along the approaches to the river twisting eastward. He sighed heavily, grateful that at last the long journey was almost over.

"How much farther to the place of the Sleeping Buffalo?" inquired a young brave, and Iron responded, "Nightfall will see us arriving there."

"This rain . . . well, it must be endured." Rocky Boy gestured toward the river and the thick underbrush there, and farther away in the breaks. "Still there is no buffalo. But we must eat. Calf Shirt, form a hunting party and look for antelope or deer."

"I will go with Calf Shirt," stated Iron.

In a matter of minutes the hunting party swept down into a ravine to disappear, and Rocky Boy kept his people on the move. When the river bent to the north, the Ojibwa knew the place they sought was only a couple of miles away, and a new spring came into their step. Coming up to ride alongside Rocky Boy was Old Washita. Washita seemed all skin and bones and dark, weathered skin, with one band of gray hair splashing over the crown of his head. He had a habit of breathing heavily through his mouth, and of spitting from time to time. His squaw, Willow That Bends, plodded along with the other women, laden with a pack lashed to her back. Some of the older children had been here before, but outriders kept them from running ahead.

Washita, in a quaking voice, said, "There is talk that Coyote Walker will seek haven with the Blackfoot."

"Then he is a fool."

A gap-toothed grin split Old Washita's wide

mouth. "Or it could be Coyote Walker will leave his scalplock there."

And then the Ojibwa were coming over an elevation and upon the place of the Sleeping Buffalo. They viewed several boulders riddling a sloping hill a short distance away from the Milk River. Of special interest to Rocky Boy and his people was a dome-shaped boulder that resembled a buffalo lying down—the famous Sleeping Buffalo. The symbolic history of the Sleeping Buffalo went back generations to when the Assinniboines first came upon the Milk River country to find the rock already well established and revered.

As the legend went, a party of Indians looking for horses sighted a herd of buffalo lying down, and crawled up to the herd only to find it turned to stone; the largest of these rocks was the "sleeping buffalo." Another legendary tale was of an Indian youth and his wife who had traveled far, searching for buffalo, but the youth had fallen sick and taken to his bed in the lodge not far from Cree crossing. His wife had gone out each day and one day was dipping water from the creek not far from the Sleeping Buffalo, when she saw a cow buffalo in the willows. She ran to get her husband, who was given strength to rise from his bed, pick up his arrows and kill the buffalo. Meat and soup from the animal brought him back to health, and ever afterward the rocks had brought good fortune to other hunters.

Now the Ojibwa, despite the pounding rain, set about making camp. While the squaws put up tepees, Chief Rocky Boy ordered his large and colorful lodge erected over the ancient sleeping

13

buffalo rock. Above the entrance to the lodge an Ojibwa medicine man had painted a buffalo's head. Later, when it stopped raining and twilight descended upon the camp, fires were started at each corner of the stone. Then the chiefs and medicine men and a few braves settled down in the lodge, with one of the medicine men chanting his rituals as he painted in new, bright colors the ancient symbols on the rock. This ritual would go on for some time, Rocky Boy knew. A shout from outside brought his eyes toward the open door of the lodge and the hunting party returning with the carcass of a mule deer slung over a horse.

Said Old Washita, "Already the spirits look with favor upon the Ojibwa."

"One deer," Rocky Boy said gravely, "will not last long. It is the buffalo we seek."

"Shall we not find them?"

"Only if the spirit of the Sleeping Buffalo listens to our prayers."

TWO

Even during the Indian Wars the daily routine of the soldiers at Fort Assinniboine was dictated by bugle calls. One lieutenant's wife remarked that she had a special affection for the stable-call for the cavalry, when the horses were groomed and watered, the thrilling fire-call and the startling assembly, or call-to-arms, when every soldier jumped for his rifle and every officer buckled on his sword, and a woman's heart stood still. But for others—the corporals and buck privates—army life was glittering misery.

"So tell me, Sergeant Murdock, why would high-and-mighty General Phil Sheridan come all the way out here to Fort Assinniboine?"

"You know as well as I do, Corporal Buckley, about these Indians being forced out of Canada."

"Policy, you mean."

"Policy—army regulations—call it what you will, Buckley. We are here merely to help protect the civilians."

15

"I also heard that if this uprising up in Canada hadn't occurred, Fort Assinniboine was going to be closed down."

"What difference does it make, Buckley, since you've still got two years to go on your enlistment. Now, how do I look?"

Both of the cavalrymen were getting ready for guard mount. Buckley checked over Sergeant Ira Murdock's dress blues and could see nothing amiss. Where the sergeant was blocky-faced but leaned to the saddle, Corporal Buckley had trouble keeping the weight off, mostly due to a fondness for beer served at the sutler's store, and for heaping his plate with extra servings at the mess hall. Their everyday work uniforms were different from the guard mount dress uniforms, with polished buttons and freshly blackened shoes. Ira Murdock was taking special pains, since one of the sergeants turning out for guard mount would be selected as orderly for General Phil Sheridan during his short visit here. This was a much-coveted assignment, for the orderly was excused from guard duty and fatigue details, and generally loafed about post headquarters when not carrying messages. The troopers called this "dog robbing," since in their opinion all the orderly ever did was hurrah the hired girl in the kitchen and get victuals reserved for officers—this, along with reflecting honor upon the sergeant, his company, and his captain.

The rat-tat-tatting of a bugle brought both of them, and three other troopers, out of the barracks to assemble there under the eyes of the company first

16

sergeant. A second bugle call about ten minutes later found the guard detail being marched over to the parade ground. Those detailed to guard mount from other barracks were coming in at march step. It was here the top-ranking enlisted man at Fort Assinniboine, Sergeant-Major J.B. Callahan, announced assignments to the various posts around the large fort. A cold and aloof martinet, Callahan was the only enlisted man wearing a sword, with yellow trimming his helmet, jacket and trousers. In a gruff voice the sergeant-major added, "'Tis you I've selected, Sergeant Murdock, to be General Sheridan's orderly. But, mon, one misstep and I'll have your stripes."

"Yessir, Sergeant-Major," responded a grinning Ira Murdock.

Pivoting on the heels of his polished boots, Sergeant-Major Callahan turned his charges over to the officer of the day, who promptly marched them away. "Come on, Murdock, quit gawking . . . for the general's waiting."

"Yo, Sergeant-Major. Just why was it you picked me, Callahan?"

"Because you're the best of a scurvy lot."

"Callahan, you always did recognize quality in a man."

"Don't push it, Murdock. You will keep me posted on anything out of the ordinary happening . . . now won't you, Sergeant Murdock?" The sergeant-major didn't wait for a reply as he entered the headquarters building ahead of Murdock and strode briskly toward his office.

With some hesitation, Sergeant Murdock traipsed down the long hallway toward a small contingent of officers clustered there. Only when a lieutenant from his company caught Murdock's eye did he feel more at ease. Detaching himself from the others, Lieutenant John J. Pershing, a tall, jut-jawed man with an erect posture, had a smile for Ira Murdock.

"So it's you, Murdock?"

"Yessir—for better or worse, sir."

"Buck up, Sergeant; the general treats everyone fairly." Pershing brought Murdock farther along to where an enlisted man stood at arms rest before an open doorway.

"Ah, Pershing," said Major Tennison upon glancing up from his desk.

In an aside to Murdock, Lieutenant Pershing stated that Tennison was General Phil Sheridan's aide-de-camp. "Sir, Sergeant Ira Murdock, of my own H Company, I might add, has been selected to be the general's orderly."

"Then he'll do." Picking up a sheaf of papers as he rose, the major added, "Time to continue the conference. Come along, gentlemen."

Sergeant Ira Murdock found himself proceeding down the hallway to a cross corridor, at the end of which were double doors opening into a large meeting room. Murdock settled onto one of the chairs in the corridor as the officers filed into the room. Then, another enlisted man standing guard closed the doors and took up his parade rest position while glancing over at the sergeant.

"You're Riley, from B Company."

"That I am, Sergeant," he said cautiously.

"Does this meeting have something to do with those Indians pouring out of Canada?"

"Can't say for sure."

But Sergeant Ira Murdock knew this was precisely why General Phil Sheridan had come up here. Beyond the closed doors Lieutenant John Pershing and the eyes of the other officers were riveted on the general seated at the head of their long table. As was his habit, General Sheridan cut to the heart of what had brought him here.

"As commandant of Fort Assinniboine, General Otis, it will be your responsibility to keep these Cree and the Chippewa under control."

"But . . . surely the Canadian government would prefer that we round these Indians up and send them back to stand trial."

"Our neighbors to the north seem reluctant to be burdened with these Indians, gentlemen. I know, the Cree are notorious horse rustlers and thieves. But until our government can work out some deal with the Canadians, our hands are tied."

"The ranchers and settlers out here won't like this, sir."

General Sheridan's probing eyes settled upon Lieutenant Pershing. He knew by heart the details of Pershing's army career, the years the soldier known as Black Jack because Pershing commanded the Tenth (Negro) Cavalry here at Fort Assinniboine, had hunted down Geronimo's renegade Apache, and pursued Zuni out of Fort Wingate. Later there was the merciless police action in the badlands of the

Dakota-Nebraska border in which his Sioux scouts looked for Indians with bad hearts, and of course there was the battle of Wounded Knee. A tough, capable soldier. One who had a reputation for not acting hastily, yet knew intimately the ways of the Plains Indians. Later he would ask that General Otis place the young lieutenant in charge of the Indian problem.

"Now let's get to that other problem," Sheridan went on. "The Department of the Army has stated its intention to abandon Fort Assinniboine. So what has just happened up in Canada will delay this for a while. Word of this must not leave this room, gentlemen. Otherwise, you'll be overrun with land speculators."

"Yes," agreed General Otis, "as the reservation is rather large. But mostly mountainous terrain . . . and probably good only for grazing cattle."

"How goes it, Lieutenant Pershing?"

Through a tentative smile John Pershing replied, "Couldn't be better, General Sheridan."

"Your 'buffalo soldiers' put on quite an exhibition yesterday."

"Sir, they're natural-born soldiers."

At military conferences of this importance, pondered Lieutenant Pershing, three-star generals did not single out lowly lieutenants. He felt a surge of pride, and would pass on the general's comments to his cavalrymen. Chancing to glance to his left, he stared briefly into the resentful eyes of Captain Morley Griffin. The captain was a fixture here at Fort Assinniboine, and Griffin commanded D Company, which was composed of white soldiers. Griffin resented the presence of the buffalo soldiers, perhaps because the man hailed from a small Georgia town. He did not care for the nickname Black Jack, bestowed upon Pershing by his Negro troopers. Pershing had a lifelong respect and admiration for the black soldier, and only an iron discipline kept him from reading off Captain Griffin. Outwardly, John Pershing presented a granitic and emotionless personality. The moments of self-doubt were few. But what was of major importance to him was that he had gained the respect of his men, and—he hoped— that of the other officers here at Fort Assinniboine.

General Sheridan, rising from his chair, brought the other officers out of theirs and to positions of attention. When the general and his staff officers swept out into the hallway, the remaining officers began discussing the gist of what had been discussed, as they clustered around General Otis. "We've had Indian problems before," said the general.

"I still say we should intercept these Cree . . . and Chippewa . . . and escort them back into Canada."

"Politics."

"Another name for foot-dragging. Meaning we mustn't offend the Canadians."

"Meanwhile, these savages will be carrying out raids against the ranchers and small settlements."

"I disagree, Captain Griffin."

"So, the esteemed Black Jack Pershing has something to add," the captain said sarcastically.

"Mostly they'll be looking for a safe haven. I expect some will venture here."

"How absurd." Around the quick smile, Captain Griffin stroked at his trim mustache. "I'm willing to wager, Pershing, that none of these red devils come skulking in here. Say, twenty silver dollars?"

"You have a bet, sir."

"Splendid—and I trust you will honor your wager."

"Captain, that will be all," cut in General Otis, his grimace of displeasure serving to dismiss his officers, while a crooking finger kept John Pershing in the room. The general waited until an orderly had closed the doors before he swung toward a nearby window giving him a view of the parade ground and the main gates, the stars and stripes fluttering under a cloudy sky. After a while he murmured, "I'll miss this."

Lieutenant Pershing nodded politely.

"Once Fort Assinniboine is closed down, Pershing, I'm submitting my retirement papers."

"Sir, I've enjoyed serving under you."

"You'll have a fine career, John. What I've just told you is between us. So—to why I singled you out, Pershing." Sparse, about five-ten, the face veined and pitted and weathered to a leathery sheen, General Conrad Otis had a tired glimmer in eyes rimmed with deep crinkles. The gray, peppery hair was cut close to the skull, the summer-issue uniform barren of any decorations, and there was a slight tremor in the hand brushing absently at a fly flittering past his eyes. "General Sheridan is quite taken with you, Pershing. So much so that he wants your Tenth Cavalry to handle this Indian problem."

"You honor us, sir."

General Otis turned to face his lieutenant. "But before we can do anything, we must put pressure upon the Canadians . . . get them to agree to let the Cree and Chippewa return. From what General Sheridan told me in private, the provincial government is interested only in arresting the leaders of this rebellion."

"This means we'll be saddled with the bulk of them. I hear some Blackfoot were involved in this."

"Yes, some were. By now they're probably back on their reservation. And you know it'll do no good to ride up there and single these braves out. You feel that the Cree, Chippewa—even some of those half-bloods led by Louis Riel will come here—"

"Chiefly for protection, just in case Canadian militia crossed the border. And just to get some beef and staples."

"Either here, or the Indian agency at Grand Marias. In any case, the responsibility for their actions falls upon our shoulders. What we don't want is another Indian war. Which could happen if the Gros Ventres and Blackfoot get involved."

"I'll tread softly, General Otis."

Leaving the general to his own thoughts, a light-footed John Pershing found his way past one of the stables and crossed the parade grounds. An assignment of this kind was generally given to a more senior officer, and he knew his being picked would stir up a lot of resentment. But the weeks of inactivity, except for a few patrols, had served to whet his appetite for the trail again. Passing through the main gates, he veered away from the main road and toward an Indian camp spilled along a creek. A dog began barking, then others, while a squaw with a distended belly wobbled out of a tepee and threw Pershing a gaptoothed grin. He tramped along a vague pathway, cutting around junipers, and went up a hump of land to come upon a lonely tepee; just beyond this lay a crumbling trapper's cabin.

This was the property of Kermit Iron Horn, one of the Arikara scouts. Smoke spewing out of the fieldstone chimney spoke of Iron Horn being in one of his civilized moods. At the age of ten the Arikara had been forced into the hands of the Jesuits, and out of this had come a bittersweet attitude toward the Black Hands and the ways of the white men. Now at an age John Pershing estimated to be between thirty and forty or so, Iron Horn had contributed greatly to the success of the Dakota-Nebraska border campaign. A loner by choice, possessed of a cynical and fatalistic nature, Kermit Iron Horn respected few white men, though he considered Pershing a friend.

This was something, pondered John Pershing, he'd learned to accept, as from creekward came a squaw's titillating laughter. With a resigned sigh, he claimed a seat on the front porch steps and reached into a tunic pocket for his briar pipe. If Iron Horn had any vices, it was his passion for Blackfoot women—a hankering that had made the Arikara a hated man in Blackfoot country. The young army lieutenant had no intention of viewing a naked Iron Horn or his squaw at the moment they partook of a late afternoon swim.

Sometime later, perhaps a good forty minutes, he

24

blinked away his thoughts to find the squaw trailing Iron Horn up the creek bank. There he was, the Arikara Iron Horn, somewhat shorter than Lieutenant Pershing at five-ten, bold of features and with black hair spilling over his wide shoulders. Iron Horn wore a plain buckskin suit and had the long stride of a man used to tracking on foot when that became necessary; there was a tentative smile for John Pershing. He'd lost the little finger of his left hand in a knife fight; other markings on his body, from both knife and lead slugs, were also a legacy of a violent life. The almond eyes regarded the white intruder with a challenging glint.

"My squaw has a friend . . ."

"That should please you immensely."

Guttural laughter split the wide lips of Iron Horn. "This one has a jealous nature. So, Pershing, can it be your coming here has to do with what is happening up in Canada?"

Pershing waited until the squaw had scurried past him into the cabin, and then he dragged on his pipe while murmuring, "Just what do you know, Kermit?"

"About as much as that juniper." Iron Horn went up the short flight of wooden steps and settled onto a backless chair as Pershing shifted on the steps to face the Arikara. "They flee south . . . the Cree, Chippewa . . . and some Blackfoot. Then what?"

"Perhaps you could tell me?"

"No, it isn't what the army thinks. Here they seek refuge . . . not war."

"My opinion of the situation."

"Then why are you here, Pershing?"

"I figure you know why."

"To find these renegades. There is an ancient crossing northeast of here . . . the Milk River." Iron Horn glanced at his horses grazing in a lush meadow. "I fear it won't be too much longer, Pershing, before your army won't need the Arikara. When I ride I see too much chimney smoke, cattle grazing on Indian land, always wagon tracks pointing to the west. This is a sad time."

"Maybe not for the best, either, Kermit. When can you leave?"

"Allow me one last night with my Blackfoot squaw."

"Keep your eyes peeled out there."

That evening found Lieutenant John Pershing attending a dress ball held to honor General Sheridan's presence here at Fort Assinniboine. The music was provided by troopers from Pershing's Tenth Cavalry, and about eight o'clock John Pershing entered the large ballroom clad in the full dress uniform of a cavalry officer: double-breasted frock coat with yellow epaulets, sash and buttons, the plumed helmet tucked under one arm. One of the few unmarried officers, he rarely attended functions of this kind, but he also realized these events helped to ease the boredom of army life. After handing his helmet to a soldier tending the cloak room, he turned to find General Sheridan's aide thrusting out a hand, and Major Tennison murmuring softly, "Congratulations, Lieutenant Pershing, on your new assignment."

"Quoting from Mark Twain—if it wasn't the honor of the thing . . ."

The major smiled and said, "In a way, I envy you. This just could be the last of our Indian problems."

"I've the feeling it's a Canadian problem thrust upon us."

"Meaning the Canadians won't allow these Cree and Chippewa to return—"

"Something of that nature."

"Lieutenant Pershing, how nice to see you again."

John Pershing turned slightly and returned the eager smile of Sallie Griffin. Perhaps in her middle twenties, this evening sheathed in a long, blue, shimmering gown with a low neckline, endowed with an oval face and widely spaced eyes and auburn hair, the young woman was the only daughter of Captain Morley Griffin. Sallie Griffin was one of the few unmarried women at the fort, and he knew some of the other officers coveted her hand. Under different circumstances he could have courted Sallie Griffin, but there was a certain woman in Wyoming who was on his mind of late, and with whom he corresponded. Hovering a short distance away were a couple of second lieutenants, and Pershing said, "As lovely as ever, Miss Griffin."

"You could honor me with the next dance?"

"Aren't you spoken for?"

"Not when you're around, John Pershing."

He found himself escorting Sallie Griffin onto the dance floor and stepping along to the tune of a waltz. They came around the huge floor and under the cold, watchful eyes of Captain Morley Griffin. But she had a smile for her father as they swept past, and she said, questioningly, "A pity my father dislikes you so, Lieutenant Pershing."

"Life is what one makes it. I certainly bear no malice toward your father."

"He came home this afternoon speaking of some wager . . ."

"Gambling is something an officer does not discuss in the presence of a beautiful woman."

"Just what do you want to talk about, John?" she said coyly.

Before John Pershing could frame a reply, his eyes and those of other officers swung to another officer hurrying across the dance floor to confer with Generals Otis and Sheridan. Now it was General Otis striding out onto the dance floor to announce the unexpected presence of rebellious half-breeds who had been driven out of Canada. "Pershing, Major Tennison, come with me. You other officers can go on with the festivities."

"John," called out a major, "seems you just won some money from the esteemed Captain Griffin."

"So it seems. Excuse me, Sallie." Retrieving his dress hat, Pershing went outside and strolled behind the generals and other officers coming onto the fringes of the parade ground, where General Sheridan pulled up abruptly. "Quite a large contingent . . . over three hundred, I'd say."

Now Lieutenant John Pershing got his first glimpse of Louis Riel and Gabriel Dumont, the leaders of the Saskatchewan Rebellion, reining their horses away from the other half-bloods and crossing toward them. About them was the look of men who had been driven to the brink of exhaustion; still, both Riel and Dumont flashed arrogant smiles as they pulled up and stared at the officers.

"So, it is from you, General Otis, that we seek sanctuary."

"Just who are you?"

"But of course. I am Louie Riel . . . the rightful ruler of Canadian land to the north."

"Gabriel Dumont," the other said disdainfully. "All we are seeking is food and supplies for our people."

"It has been reported to me," snapped General Otis, "that you and your half-bloods killed and burned their way across the province. I'll see that your people are given food. But as of this moment, Mr. Riel . . . and Mr. Dumont . . . you're under military arrest. Pershing, take charge of their weapons."

As John Pershing stepped forward, Louis Riel sawed back angrily on the reins and said, "We have broken no laws down here."

"Let's just say, Riel, that I have no choice in the matter. We will take care of your people."

"Does this mean Dumont and I will be handed over to the damned British?"

General Phil Sheridan replied, "For the time being, you men will be treated no differently from any other foreigners requesting asylum. But you must understand that what happened in Canada is of grave concern to the War Department. There is every possibility you could be considered political refugees. But for the time being we have no choice but to detain you gentlemen."

Conflicting emotions rippled across Louis Riel's swarthy face as he twisted in the saddle and glanced at his ragtag army. They had been defeated decisively at the battle of Batoche, but not without severe loss of life to Canadian militia. The Canadians had been nipping at their heels when they crossed the border into Montana. Briefly, he stared at Dumont, and down at John Pershing; then he unsheathed his rifle. Thrusting it at Pershing, Louis Riel said bitterly, "Much to my sorrow, it is over."

"Sir, what happened to the Cree and Blackfoot Indians . . . those who fought with you?"

"I am no longer concerned with them. When the Canadians attacked us, they fled. Perhaps down here, or northward into the Northwest Territories."

At a curt command from Pershing, his prisoners dismounted, to be escorted by an armed guard away from the parade grounds and toward the post stockade. A short distance behind came John Pershing, with the troubling knowledge in him that this was far from over. It was his feeling that Riel and Dumont had exploited the Indians, and possibly his half-breeds. Now all of this had become an American problem, with John Pershing and his Tenth Cavalry caught in the middle of it. The next step would be to locate those scattered bunches of Indians who had fled south, something that he was absolutely certain Kermit Iron Horn could handle. Afterwards it all depended on the sometimes uncertain whims of the War Department. If what he had learned at the briefing was fact—that the Canadian government was reluctant to have either Louis Riel's half-bloods or the Cree, Chippewa and Blackfoot, forcibly escorted back into Canada—this could turn into an explosive situation. In these parts, ranchers and settlers still carried the scars and bitter memories of the Indian Wars so recently ended.

I fear, Lieutenant Pershing said to himself, there'll be trouble—even some bloodshed—before long. And all because of Riel's vainglorious dream.

THREE

It still wasn't clear to Wilfred Haley why he had been summoned to Secretary Josh Tremont's home on this rainy spring night, then dispatched from there on this somewhat clandestine errand. After all, there were higher ranking officials working for the Indian Office in the War Department. But in his year and a half of servitude, as Haley called it, one went along with the flow or sought employment elsewhere. A barrister, and a graduate of Harvard, Wilfred Haley enjoyed working here in Washington City. However, at the moment he was having misgivings about this shabby sector of the city and the fact that his carriage had just left the streetlights behind and was clattering over the uneven cobblestones of a street lined by dark warehouses and vacant lots. When a wheel found a chuckhole, Haley's cane rapped against the front window.

"Careful, you black—"

Remembrance of where he was brought him back against the seat cushions as an unsteady hand flitted into an inner coat pocket for the flask. As he drank, the young lawyer spared neither his resentment toward Secretary Tremont nor the brandy. He'd heard this was a section of the city frequented by pickpockets, petty thieves, and worse. Just how far could he trust his Negro driver?

Finally, though it had taken less than an hour, the carriage rolled onto a wider street, and Haley's driver announced they were approaching notorious Old Capital Prison. Lifting the side curtain, Haley blinked out at a high brick courtyard. Then the carriage swung into a driveway and drew up before an arched doorway. With a grimace, its passenger stepped down onto muddy ground. He hunkered into his belted coat while hurrying up to the door to pound a clenched fist against the thick wooden pane.

"Come on," he muttered impatiently.

A slot in the door scraped open. "Mr. Haley?"

"But of course."

The door swung open, leaving Wilfred Haley just enough room to squeeze through. He gave the guard a jaundiced eye as the man closed and bolted the door, leaving Haley a moment to stare about the large courtyard with some trepidation. "Isn't this . . . ?"

"Where they hung the Lincoln conspirators? This very courtyard. To the west there, just this side of the wall. This way, Mr. Haley."

Vivid images of the newspaper pictures he'd seen commemorating that historic event hung like a dark cloud in Haley's thoughts. The high wooden scaffold . . . some guards standing higher on the back wall . . . dangling to the left, Mrs. Surratt; then Lewis Paine, Atzerodt, Herold. With a mingling of soldiers and civilians about where Wilfred Haley was walking at the moment. Damn fools, he mused.

Before him loomed the main prison, the bricks whitewashed to the bottoms of the second-story windows, a wet and mottled red from there upward to the peaked and chimneyed roof. No lights showed, making the vast structure look as empty as the Great Plains now that the great buffalo herds were gone. At their approach, a door creaked open, and Haley had no choice but to proceed ahead of his escort into a dreary corridor lighted by one lamp.

"Your papers?"

"Wha . . ." he stammered, adding, "I didn't see you standing there." With some hesitation he reached into a coat pocket for the manila envelope given him by Secretary Tremont.

Disdainful of the seal closing the envelope, the stranger, a somewhat burly man crammed into a rumpled brown suit, tore an end away and spilled out its contents. "Yes, this will suffice."

"Well, sir, you have your letter. Now where's that parcel I'm supposed to pick up?"

"Bring out the prisoner!"

"What devilment is this?"

One of the guards shuffled over and unlocked a cell door. Opening it, he gestured wearily to its shadowy occupant, who came out hesitantly. The man in the rumpled suit told Wilfred Haley that his next order of business was to escort his "parcel" to Union Station.

Haley took in the wrist irons, the rather gaunt and longish face and the pale, bluish eyes which, as Haley's did, glimmered bewilderedly. "What . . . what kind of game is this?"

"Let's just say, Mr. Haley, that certain cogs and gears have been greased: the way of it here in Washington City. Would you prefer we remove the irons?"

"No!" he blurted out. "What crime has this man been charged with?"

"Sorry, but that's no concern of yours. Snyder, escort Mr. Haley and his parcel out to their carriage."

Wilfred Haley heard the outer courtyard door slam shut and found himself alone with his prisoner, a man of about the same age, but a trifle taller at six feet, sandy-haired, the suit which he'd probably worn when imprisoned now draped loosely over the angular frame. The light-colored beard was unkempt, as was the shaggy hair spilling from under the shapeless felt hat. When his prisoner flashed a sudden smile, Haley caught a glimpse of bone-shiny teeth, and there was a moment of anxiety.

"I'm rather a hungry parcel, Mr. Haley."

"Ah," Haley exclaimed nervously, "that's no concern of mine."

"I could make a break for it." Saying this, the prisoner unleashed another smile for the colored driver, whose teeth were bared in the black, rain-spattered face. "You have all the mannerisms of a lawyer, Haley. Which I am . . . or was. Aaron Wilkerson at your service."

"This rain doesn't seem to be letting up. Perhaps

we should avail ourselves of my carriage." Haley opened the carriage door and motioned for his prisoner to get inside, which the man did somewhat stiffly, as though he'd suffered cruel punishment or an inadequate diet. Wilfred Haley piled in and clicked the door shut.

Wilkerson said, "I don't suppose you have the keys for these?"

"No. I forgot to ask." The carriage lurched ahead. "Look, Wilkerson, I don't know what this is all about. My instructions were simply to pick up a parcel at Old Capital Prison. Which I've done. You're most certainly not a . . . a parcel. Nor have I any idea why I have to take you to Union Station." He found the flask. "Here, this might drive away some of the chill."

"Your accent bespeaks . . . Boston."

"Actually, Cape Cod."

"Yes, the money crowd."

"We were well off," Haley said crossly.

"But now you're trafficking in convicts—"

"I dare say, sir, I have an honorable position here in Washington City. Now, if you please, I have a headache."

Aaron Wilkerson turned his eyes and thoughts to the passing streets. Haley, he concluded, was just an errand boy. Business of the court generally took place during daylight hours, but whoever had dispatched Wilfred Haley to Old Capital Prison was someone of importance. Could it be that one of his former partners was behind this? Or perhaps others who'd been involved in that land fraud down in Georgia? For his part in the land scheme, Aaron Wilkerson had been sentenced to serve ten years. Another idea formed in his embittered thoughts, and he let it simmer for a few moments before murmuring inwardly, This could be an attempt on my life. But why, since I was just one of the minor characters in that land scheme?

He was still puzzling over this when their carriage rolled around a corner to turn onto a wide boulevard. By now he'd emptied the flask, and didn't realize he was holding it until it slipped out of his grasp. Reaching down, he tossed it next to him on the padded seat. He flicked a studied glance at his seat companion. A lawyer, Haley had stated. Which meant Wilfred Haley could be working for some department of the federal government.

"At last, Union Station."

"So it is," agreed Aaron Wilkerson. "By chance, Mr. Haley, you wouldn't be employed by the government?"

"Why do you ask?"

"The way you were able to extract me from that prison. Well?"

Haley said smugly, "As a matter of fact I am— Department of the Interior."

There it was, the connection to a man he suspected was behind the land scheme. Anger lidded Aaron Wilkerson's eyes as their carriage swung to the curb. More than anger—a terrible hatred that bunched the muscles along his jawbone. At that moment he wanted to lash out at Haley with his wrist manacles, inflict great pain and hurt in an attempt to get at the

38

truth. The bitterness passed as he set his mind on his only living relative. He could still remember coming to this city and looking up Uncle Josh, and how Josh Tremont had gotten him a job in some obscure government department. Later there had come the invitation to visit Tremont's palatial Washington home, to mingle briefly with people he read about daily in the newspapers. Until one day, through Tremont, Aaron Wilkerson had secured a high position with the prestigious land firm of Bailey & Addison. Eighteen months passed, and then Aaron was suddenly arrested, along with others working for Bailey & Addison, and charged with land fraud. Since he had little money for an adequate defense, his trial had been a mere formality, followed by months behind bars. Now tonight, and the unexpected appearance of Haley. Could it be that he was an embarrassment to Josh Tremont as long as he was imprisoned here in Washington? That his influential uncle had arranged his transfer to another prison?

Whatever it is, Aaron told himself, it bodes no good for me.

The door sprang open and their driver announced, "Mr. Haley, suh, here's the train depot."

"What now?" muttered Wilfred Haley as he eased outside.

"I believe there's some gentlemen coming out of the depot, suh."

"Must be here to meet us. You'd better dismount, Wilkerson."

Sliding over, Aaron swung a leg down onto the step, followed that by crouching outside and staring toward two men advancing across the wide sidewalk running along Union Station. The one in the derby hat took the toothpick out of his mouth and said to Haley, "We'll take it from here." A grateful and puzzled Wilfred Haley climbed back into his carriage and watched as Aaron Wilkerson was forcibly escorted into Union Station.

The depot was familiar territory to Aaron Wilkerson, although he could do without being hustled past the Negro porters slouching near the sidings and huge carts ready to be used when a train ground to a stop. He half expected to be on that train when it departed—or another. Both of his escorts were barely a cut above prison guards—quiet men with scowling faces that prompted him to say, "Just where are we going, gentlemen?"

After a few moments, Derby Hat mumbled, "You'll find out soon enough." His grip tightened on Aaron Wilkerson's arm as they veered into a dark, narrow hallway. The wrist irons were removed, with Derby Hat opening his coat to reveal the holstered gun. "You're expected; second door on the right. Any farther than that, Wilkerson, and we gun you down."

Rubbing his chafed wrists, he forced a quick smile and turned to shuffle down the hallway. There was the clacking of a hammer being thumbed back when he reached the designated door. Vague light reflected through the glass pane in the door. A glance to his left revealed Derby Hat leveling his revolver. Why all this secrecy, Uncle Josh, he pondered bitterly. At first he hadn't been all that certain, but after months in prison the inescapable conclusion had come to

Aaron Wilkerson that in some way Secretary Josh Tremont was connected to the land scheme. Until he had come to Washington City, Aaron had known little about his uncle, other than the fact that Josh Tremont had been a successful businessman before becoming involved with the government. Vain, arrogant, deceitful, Uncle Josh was all of these and more. These, and the term heart-of-stone fit nicely. Get on with it.

Tugging at the brim of his hat, Aaron turned the knob and swung the door open. He stepped into the small office, only to see a man he didn't know swing up from behind a desk. "About time you got here. Step to that wall and assume the position."

"I don't understand."

"Just," the man said gruffly, "want to make sure you ain't carrying a knife . . . or handgun. Come on, it's getting late." He waited until Aaron had stepped up to the wall and leaned against it before searching for a weapon. "Okay, you're clean." He jerked a thumb toward an inner office door. "The man who wants to see you is in there. Come, come."

The inner office, Aaron Wilkerson discovered, was as sparsely furnished as the outer one, but in it, behind the only desk, stood a man he'd learned to hate and distrust. Coldly his eyes played over Josh Tremont's expensive clothing, the manicured hands heavy with glittering diamond rings, the fawning smile on the chubby face.

"Well, nephew, we meet again. Please, sit down. I'll try to make this brief, as we haven't too much time until your train leaves."

41

"My train . . . to take me to another prison . . . damn you."

"Now, Aaron, I can understand your anger. But what could I do? According to the reports I received, they caught you redhanded . . . you and some others. But all that's changed."

Wilkerson removed his hat and slumped onto a chair facing the desk. Josh Tremont sat down and smiled again. "I got you out of prison for good reason, Aaron."

"So that I can get involved in some more crooked schemes!"

"Young man," Tremont said icily, "consider this. One word from me and you're back in Old Capital Prison—to serve out the rest of your rather long jail sentence." He reached down and lifted a leather valise to place it on the desk.

Somehow Aaron subdued the temper that had always gotten him into trouble. Somehow he knew that what Uncle Josh had in mind for him wasn't a transfer to another prison. He listened attentively as Josh Tremont told him that he wanted his nephew to head west for territorial Montana and take over as Indian agent.

Hearing this, Aaron exclaimed, "Indian agent? The only Indians I know are the wooden kind. Why, I haven't been west of . . . of Pennsylvania."

"This will be a splendid opportunity for you, Aaron." He took some papers out of the valise. "I have detailed just what I want you to do. When you arrive at Havre . . . that's in Montana . . . there'll be a gentleman waiting to give you every assistance."

"Montana," he spat out. "What insanity is this? No . . . I prefer going back to prison."

"Which is where you'll be, Aaron my boy, but with time added onto your sentence for breaking out of prison. I can arrange this very easily. Damnit, boy, there's a lot of money to be made out there . . . for both of us. And I need someone out there I can trust."

"Trust? You dare speak to me of trust!"

"I'm also speaking to you, Aaron, of a chance to get away from Washington City. A chance to begin a new life. You must know that as head of the Indian Bureau I control a lot of western land. But to control not only a vast chunk of land but a lot of unruly Indians, I must have men I can trust."

"You said there's a lot of money to be made out there . . ."

"The reason I'm asking you to go to Montana. Very well, I'll lay some of my cards on the table. In the very near future the army plans to abandon Fort Assinniboine Military Reservation. This land could be sold to speculators, or, from what I've heard, made into another Indian reservation."

"Don't you have the final word on this?"

"Congress does, my boy."

"If I hear you right," Aaron said, "you stand nothing to gain if this land is given to the Indians."

"I always said you were a bright young man."

"What if I took what I've just learned to . . . say, a congressman . . ."

"It would be my word against that of an escaped felon. Surely you can see that, my boy."

"All I see is that you've got me boxed in."

43

Framing a soothing smile, Secretary Josh Tremont dropped a hand into the valise and took out a thick stack of greenbacks. "Five thousand for starters, Aaron. To get you settled out there. And to buy some new clothing. I take it you'll be leaving for Montana?"

"Only," Aaron Wilkerson said savagely, "to get away from you and this miserable town."

"That's being sensible, my boy. When you reach Havre, Aaron, you'll be contacted by a Mr. Kirby. I'm sure you two gentlemen will get along splendidly. And speaking of getting along"—from a vest pocket Josh Tremont took out his turnip-shaped watch—"your train leaves in fifteen minutes."

"Just like that," he said bitterly. "I could skip out when the train gets to Chicago—"

"Perhaps. But how far can you go on the money I've given you? No, my boy, you'll go to Havre. No question about that. Otherwise, really, my boy, I'd surely dislike sending the law after you . . . which you know I'll most certainly do."

When the train pulled out of Union Station, a chastened Aaron Wilkerson sat staring out a window at the scattering of city lights slowly fading away. Just leaving Washington City behind helped chase away a lot of bitter feelings and memories. But he felt that Secretary Josh Tremont and his bullyboys were with him on this train, and would accompany him on that long journey to territorial Montana—to him an alien place, full of savagery and untamed areas. Let tomorrow take care of tomorrow, for Montana was a whole world away. First there would be a layover at Chicago, for a new wardrobe and a night on the town.

"Then it'll be Montana," he murmured. Rising, he passed into the pullman car and found his berth. "There I'll be doing more of Secretary Tremont's crooked work—if some renegade Blackfoot doesn't kill me first."

FOUR

In the week Rocky Boy and the Ojibwa Chippewa had been camped along the Milk River, others came straggling in—mostly small bunches of Cree and some Blackfoot. As best they could, the Chippewa had given shelter and food to these newcomers. Though hunting parties had gone out, to the south and eastward along the river, no buffalo were found, but they did bring back deer and antelope. The women and children went about gathering wild plant foods; a birchwood digging stick was used for collecting bitterroot or camass bulbs. Often the children would cut away the cottonwood trees until they could suck out the sweet inner bark. Prairie chickens, wild geese, ducks, curlews, and game birds also provided the food staple of Rocky Boy's people.

Fortunately for the Chippewa, the summery weather held in the low seventies, but even the pleasant, clear days failed to chase away Rocky Boy's worries. Along with the medicine men, he had secluded himself in his lodge and prayed many times to the spirit of the Sleeping Buffalo. Three days later he had emerged from his lodge to find Old Washita crouched near his small campfire.

"If there are any buffalo left," said Rocky Boy, "surely they would have reached the Milk River by now."

"We knew a couple of summers ago that the day of the great herds is over. Perhaps it is true that some buffalo are out there."

Rocky Boy eased down, settled his legs under him, and with a nod took the hunk of venison from his friend. "As you say, Washita, there could be buffalo farther south. Surely not up in Canada. I see that some of those Cree have left camp."

"Along with those Blackfoot. Fewer mouths to feed."

"What of Little Bear?"

"He could have been captured by the Canadian soldiers."

"If so, he would not give up without a struggle . . . This is very good."

"Not as rib-sticking as buffalo."

"Here is what the Chippewa must do. I do not know how long we can camp here without being driven off."

"This land belongs to the Indian," Washita said firmly.

"Not according to reports brought back by those out looking for deer or antelope. To the east, southward, even to the west they have seen a lot of cattle. Sometimes white men on horseback. They have also come upon a few settlements. So I fear we must do as has been done in Canada—make our presence known to the soldiers. Perhaps east at Fort Belknap."

"In case you've forgotten, Rocky Boy, there are no soldiers over there. It is an Indian agency now . . . for Assinniboine and the Sioux."

"But if we go there, the Indian agent must give us cattle and staples . . . perhaps give the Chippewa some land."

"It would be more like that Indian agent to have us arrested. Afterwards we would be taken back to Canada and handed over to their soldiers."

"Whatever it is," Rocky Boy said wearily. "Another week, perhaps, and there will be no more game, at least around here. This land is too open." He swung a languid hand to the vague humps of mountains to the west. "There are the mountains, land unknown to us. Game would be plentiful there, Washita, and even the white men dare not claim those heights."

"The Blackfoot claim that land. I fear they will never welcome us as brothers."

"Just a sad notion, my friend."

Some of the dogs chose that moment to cut loose with a yowling crescendo, emptying the lodges as a small band of horsemen topped a distant rise. Both of the chiefs, Rocky Boy and Old Washita, rose and eyed perhaps two dozen Cree loping in along the river. They were, Rocky Boy realized, the band of Little Bear. Some of the Cree rode slumped in their saddles, and as they approached, it became apparent that these Indians had sustained wounds in their fight against Canadian soldiers. In a way, Rocky Boy resented the presence of these Cree. Had they not joined with the Meti, the Chippewa would still be on their ancestral lands in Canada. Rocky Boy stood there as the arrivals were greeted by his people, and as the Cree, Little Bear, rode his war pony over and stared down solemnly at his uncle, muttering tiredly, "Are we welcome in the camp of Rocky Boy?" Little Bear had a high, bulging forehead and wide-flaring nose above a downturned mouth, and black hair hanging in braids over his shoulders.

Gesturing for Little Bear to dismount, Rocky Boy said, "I see you came from the east."

"We sought help," the Cree said bitterly, "at Fort Belknap. Instead, there was more trouble. Some of the Assinniboine tried to steal our horses. So, in a brief fight, one of them was killed."

"Always there is trouble," intoned Old Washita. "But I will let the nephew of Rocky Boy eat at my fire."

Rocky Boy settled down with the others. He knew that Little Bear had been an instigator of the Frog Lake massacre, where every man in the village had been killed except one. There had been other battles involving Little Bear's Cree. For the time being he would give Little Bear sanctuary. His greatest fear was of the Canadians either sending troops down or requesting that the U.S. Army arrest the hostiles—Louis Riel's Meti and his Chippewa, the Cree, and the Blackfoot, and bring them back to Canada to stand trial in a white man's court of law.

"What happened to the half-bloods?"

"Riel's Meti?" Little Bear said scornfully. "When they saw the battle was lost, those half-bloods fled so swiftly not even their shadows could catch up. Now Riel has become my enemy, for, by listening to his sweet talk, the Cree have lost everything."

"You still live."

"As an outcast."

"What about your women and children?"

Little Bear reached over with his hunting knife and sliced away a hunk of venison from a large piece of hindquarter roasting on a spit. "For the moment it is better they remain up north. First we must make a new home down here."

"That will be difficult."

"I will take my Cree and call upon the Blackfoot. They have much land. I hear game is plentiful there, too."

"A selfish race, Little Bear. Do you not know that much of the Blackfoot land has been taken away? Now they are forced to live on a reservation . . . as are all the other tribes down here. I feel that if the American government can cede land to these tribes, why should they not help us . . . even your Cree."

"How can Little Bear and his people live on a reservation? We are not farmers, which is what these other tribes have become. Worse than that, my uncle—they no longer know how to fight. To steal horses. Cattle. To be men."

"Dangerous talk down here," said Old Washita.

"Not for Little Bear. The Cree are still a people to be reckoned with. So . . . there is Coyote Walker. I must have a word with him. My uncle, Old Washita, we will leave soon so as not to become unnecessary burdens for the Chippewa."

"To join the Blackfoot?"

"Perhaps. Or to see the Rockies again."

Waiting until Little Bear had stepped around a

tepee, Rocky Boy picked up a small twig and traced an errant pattern in the dusty ground at his feet. "Some," he finally said, "never learn."

"I fear trouble clings to your nephew."

"A sad thing. Since the Cree look to Little Bear for leadership. He must see the error of his ways before it is too late."

"Your nephew's talking to Coyote Walker won't help things."

"You can reason with Little Bear—though at the moment he is suffering the humiliation of being driven out of Canada. It is the Ojibwa I am worried about—Coyote Walker. This one has a black heart."

"You are chief of the Ojibwa," Old Washita reminded him. "If Coyote Walker causes any more trouble, banish him from our people."

"Perhaps," said Rocky Boy. In leaving, he thanked his old friend for the venison. Then he returned to his lodge. Crouching inside, he found that both of his wives, and the medicine men, were gone. He reached out to touch the sacred rock, the Sleeping Buffalo. He found that it brought no solace, no answer to all of the troubling questions.

Lieutenant John J. Pershing, riding alongside Sergeant Ira Murdock of his Tenth Cavalry, was intimately acquainted with this stretch of the Great Plains spilling south of the Milk River. Just a horse length behind came the Arikara scout, Kermit Iron Horn, who had sent the other scouts ahead to warn them about any approaching Cree or Ojibwa Chippewa. Pershing's buffalo soldiers trailed behind in a column of twos strung back along the fringe of trail. Just to the north of the cavalrymen the Great Northern Railroad right-of-way fringed the river. Around noon a train had passed them on its way to Havre and points farther west. The sun had traversed still farther west, until now it cast long shadows away from trees and the mounted column.

As was his habit, John Pershing clenched his briar pipe between his teeth, removing it at times to point out various landmarks or chat briefly with Sergeant Murdock. Before leaving Fort Assinniboine, he had briefed his sergeants on the report brought back to him by Iron Horn. For two days, Iron Horn had told Pershing, he had scouted out the camp of Rocky Boy, mostly to watch the comings and goings of the Cree and the few Blackfoot forced to flee Canada.

"According to Iron Horn," said Pershing, "the Chippewa are more concerned with finding something to eat than causing any trouble down here."

"They've got women and children in their camp. It's the Cree I wouldn't turn my back on, sir."

"They're notorious horse thieves."

"Name an Indian tribe that isn't. Now that the buffalo are ancient history, sir, it could be they'll turn their eyes upon cattle. Plenty of them hereabouts."

"If they do, Murdock, we'll have to contend with a lot of unhappy ranchers."

"Guess, sir, this means when it finally comes right down to it, the U.S. Army'll wind up feeding these Indians."

Kermit Iron Horn spurred up alongside Pershing, saying tersely, "Two miles to that Indian camp." Then, as if heralding his words, the pair of scouts he had sent out came loping through a draw and back toward the column. "We'll have to cross the river to get there."

"Getting onto dusk," speculated Pershing. "A bad time to ride into any Indian camp. But that full moon just coming over those hills will give us some edge."

"Sir," threw in Sergeant Murdock, "the Chippewa know if they give us any trouble it'll be back to Canada for them."

"There's always a hothead or two," responded John Pershing. "Kermit, when we ride into that camp, I want you and your scouts to keep your eyes peeled for any Cree or Blackfoot." Lieutenant Pershing left it at that, for what he hadn't told Iron Horn or his troopers was the desire of the Canadian government to have the leaders of the rebellion arrested and sent back to stand trial. He had received no direct orders from General Otis to arrest these men—just that the Tenth Cavalry was to make its presence known.

"The spiritual leader of the Chippewa is Chief Rocky Boy," Iron Horn informed them. "Because the squaws and children are with them, I do not believe the Chippewa fought with Riel against the Canadians."

"Makes sense," pondered the young lieutenant. "Could be the Canadians ordered the Chippewa out just to make a clean sweep of things."

The distant glow of campfires brought Lieutenant Pershing's cavalrymen toward the river. Once they had crossed the railroad tracks, all that stood between them and the Chippewa encampment was a high bank and scattered cottonwoods. Deliberately Persh-

54

ing revealed himself and those at the head of the column before his hand signal brought them reining up. At this point there was a river crossing; on the opposite side were a few boulders and lodges and tepees spread here and there, and Chippewa braves uneasily eying the soldiers. "Sergeant," he said quietly, "I want the men spread out in a line to either side."

Iron Horn said, "Perhaps it would be better if I went in and talked to Rocky Boy."

Nodding in agreement, John Pershing said, "The two of us will cross over." He waited until his buffalo soldiers had deployed to both sides along the high riverbank, and when Sergeant Murdock rode back, Pershing added, "Murdock, wait until we've reached the far bank before you bring your men across. Do it easy and slow. Then hold along the far bank while Iron Horn and I have a little powwow with the Chippewa."

"Sounds kind of risky, sir."

"I've found that a little restraint goes a long way toward letting a person keep his scalplock."

The next moment Pershing and Kermit Iron Horn were splashing across the shallow waters of the Milk. Along with his army-issue revolver, the lieutenant carried a seven-shot Spencer rifle, while those under his command had as their primary weapon the Springfield. Grasping the saddle horn as his cavalry mount struggled up the muddy bank, he glanced at Iron Horn and murmured quietly, "Not a very cordial welcome."

"At least, Pershing," grunted Iron Horn, "the squaws aren't throwing rocks at us." But yelping dogs converged on the pair of riders walking their horses into the small encampment of the Chippewa. Unlike John Pershing, the Arikara Iron Horn could pick out a few Cree and some Blackfoot amid the Ojibwa warriors. "I see some of my old friends are here."

"You mean a few Blackfoot."

"And some Cree. That bigger lodge . . . the square-faced Chippewa standing there is Rocky Boy."

Lieutenant John Pershing coolly threw glances back at glowering eyes as he drew up his horse beside one of the boulders strewn over the angling hillock. He stayed in the saddle for a moment, sensing there would be no trouble from the Chippewa. As he swung down, he glanced back to see his buffalo soldiers seated astride their horses on the near riverbank, with their rifles still in their scabbards.

"Kermit, you will be so kind as to tell Rocky Boy we come here seeking the cooperation of his people."

Iron Horn, who had also dismounted, closed the distance to within a few feet and spoke to Rocky Boy.

"You will also tell Rocky Boy that his people must promise not to steal cattle and horses. Tell the honorable Rocky Boy that we will give them beef and food staples once they reach Fort Assinniboine."

"I understand," Rocky Boy said falteringly, "as I speak some of the white man's words. Perhaps . . . Pershing . . . you can tell the Chippewa where to find the buffalo . . ."

Iron Horn broke in. "There are no more buffalo, up here or anyplace along the Great Plains. A sad thing . . . but this is why the Chippewa must come to

Fort Assinniboine.''

"Why must the Chippewa go to the white man's fort?"

The eyes of Pershing and Iron Horn pivoted to center on a Chippewa warrior elbowing his way past some medicine men to glower at the intruders and at Rocky Boy. "Coyote Walker says the Chippewa will go where they want . . . to hunt and to live."

A sad anger filtered into Rocky Boy's eyes. "Only if we dare go back to our ancestral lands will that happen. Here we must pay homage to a new government and laws. Can you not see, Coyote Walker, that our people suffer?"

"Only because you have become an old woman!"

"They suffer," countered Rocky Boy, "because hotheads such as you . . . and the Cree and Blackfoot . . . fought with the Meti."

"True words," Old Washita threw in.

"Then," shouted Coyote Walker, "let those of the Chippewa who want to take handouts from the soldiers, go to Fort Assinniboine. I and my followers no longer want to stay with cowards and old women. We go!" In leaving, subchief Coyote Walker paused long enough to let his eyes, full of hate, play over John Pershing and Iron Horn. Then, whirling, he pushed through the crowd of Chippewa and was gone.

"Coyote Walker," Rocky Boy said wearily, "has not learned that the warring days are over. Perhaps he never will. As for the Chippewa, Pershing, we will come to your fort. And after that . . . the Chippewa will try to find a new home."

In the evening, while bivouacked westward along

the Milk River, Iron Horn spoke boldly of how they could still expect trouble from some of the Chippewa and from Little Bear and his Cree. "They cannot return to Canada; this we know, Pershing."

"Which means they'll be looking for a place to hang their warbonnets down here."

"But where? Surely not among the Blackfoot . . . or Assinniboine or Sioux. Outcasts is what they have become. Which can only mean trouble for you, Pershing—and ranchers and settlers."

"Trouble is part of a soldier's life, Kermit. What I'm hoping is that when Fort Assinniboine is closed down, a large chunk of that land can be turned into a reservation for these Indians. And, Kermit, tomorrow I want you to go looking for those Cree."

"Little Bear and his Cree fought with those Meti. I doubt if they'll come in easily."

"Just so they don't start stealing horses and cattle again. That happens, we could have an Indian war on our hands."

"That stirs my blood, Pershing."

"I'm beginning to think you're as uncivilized as that Chippewa back there—that Coyote Walker—"

"I gave up praying with the beads a long time ago."

"How about taking scalps . . . or stealing Blackfoot women?"

"All civilized men have a few vices." Iron Horn's chortle caused him to spill a little coffee from his tin cup.

"Yup, I can see a little book learning wasn't wasted on the likes of you, Kermit. In any case, watch your backside out there."

"And you'll be?"

"Reporting back to Fort Assinniboine. Just maybe, this Louis Riel can tell us where to find those Cree." Clenching the briar pipe between his teeth with a smile, John Pershing headed for his bedroll and what he knew would be a troubled sleep.

FIVE

Perhaps if Aaron Wilkerson had known his destiny would be entwined with that small band of Ojibwa Chippewa trekking westward just across the narrow expanse of the Milk River he would have caught the next train back east. Along with his fellow passengers aboard the Great Northern passenger train, he took in the spotted ponies and travoises and regalia of the Indians, and felt a surge of excitement.

"What are they, Sioux?"

"Nope, since the Sioux are living on reservations. Could be some of those Indians that hightailed out of Canada."

"Bet you're right, Cornfield."

The carpetbagger's grin took in those seated with him, and a buxom woman across the aisle, as he said to Aaron Wilkerson, "Won't see a sight like that traipsing around Washington City."

"Or around Chicago, for that matter," Aaron replied. Beyond the Red River of the North there had been a land change, subtle at first, until their Great

Northern passenger train had crossed the Missouri River. Westward from there, flat-crowned mesas and rocky elevations broke the undulating spill of the prairie. Harbored as he had been by the forests of the East, and its large cities, this western openness of high and endless sky and vast plains aroused in Aaron Wilkerson an untamed side he hadn't known existed. As did that band of Indians, the few cowhands in the passenger car, and that flinty-eyed gent seated yonder with the outline of his .45 Peacemaker lifting the bottom of his buckskin coat. Shredding away were misconceptions he'd read about the West in eastern newspapers, though in him still burned the damning anger toward Josh Tremont.

Now the conductor called out, "Havre's our next stop—be there in fifteen minutes."

"About time," groused the carpetbagger, and to Aaron, "Yessir, this is a place of high skies and sudden death. Quite unlike what you've been used to."

"What kind of a place is Havre?"

"Just sprouting its wings; railroad town." The carpetbagger lifted an inquiring eye. "Never said what brought you out here, Wilkerson."

"Opportunity," Aaron replied as he stepped out into the aisle and headed back to the sleeper car.

The journey of more than a month had helped Aaron Wilkerson regain his self-assurance, and the weight lost while serving time in prison. The new clothing—mostly durable suits in browns and grays, told his fellow passengers that here was a young man of modest means. In Chicago he had seen the newspaper advertisement extolling the many wonders of the Oregon Territory. Enroute, he had considered heading out that way. Overriding this were the threats of Secretary Josh Tremont of the Bureau of Indian Affairs. And Aaron's decision to play out the hand dealt him and become an Indian agent.

"If Uncle Josh sees an opportunity to make a profit out of this," he murmured, "so shall his esteemed nephew." He entered his compartment and hefted the large valise, a smaller one containing a few personal items, and the handgun he had purchased at Fargo. Then he found the front door of the sleeper car while eying through the windows the wooden frame and brick buildings of this western town.

Descending the vestibule steps, Aaron Wilkerson stepped across the wooden platform fronting the depot, to get his bearings. As he had expected, the main thoroughfare cut a straight line to the west along the railroad right-of-way. From there, the spacious western town spilled away to the south in a web of streets and buildings. The carpetbagger, Cornfield, had spoken of a few fancy hotels and places of the night—saloons, dance halls, and gambling casinos. But Aaron Wilkerson's thoughts were elsewhere: perhaps Uncle Josh's agent—the man called Kirby—would put in an appearance. Along with the money, there had been some papers telling Aaron what would be expected of him. For starters, he would become the new Indian agent at Fort Belknap. Settle in there and get accustomed to the ways out here while the fate of Fort Assinniboine Military Reservation was being determined in Congress.

"Every red cent I've got left, that Uncle Josh will

corrupt some of those on that congressional committee.''

From a second-story window Aaron Wilkerson studied passengers dismounting from a Bryce & Morgan stagecoach. The stageline, he'd found out, serviced cowtowns scattered to the south. Havre's first name had been Bull Hook Siding, after Bull Hook Creek, which entered the Milk River here. The officious-looking document he was holding had been waiting for him at the post office when he arrived. The document told of his appointment as Indian agent at the Fort Belknap agency and explained some of the duties he would be performing.

But where was Mr. Kirby?

Aaron had been here almost three days—not that he hadn't enjoyed partaking of the gaming action—but his instincts as a lawyer dictated that he tend to business first. An impatient hand lifted the small glass of brandy from the only table in his hotel room. Last night he'd gotten lucky in a poker game at the Crystal Bar. As had a drifting gambler who had been accused of double-dealing by a muleskinner. There had been a flash of steel blade, the gambler palming a Derringer, but a fraction too late, as the muleskinner's knife punched into his chest. An unnerved Aaron Wilkerson had managed to blunder out the back door, where he vomited away his fear. His first order of business this morning was at a gunshop, where he purchased a shoulder holster for the Hammond breechloading revolver. It served to give Aaron back some of his self-esteem when he resumed his search

64

for the elusive Mr. Kirby.

"Perhaps," he debated, "Kirby plans to contact me at the agency."

Through the open window he glimpsed a surrey passing downstreet; the man sawing at the reins was an army officer, but it was the way the summery breeze ruffled the young woman's hair that held Aaron's eye. Could be the officer's wife, but something told him otherwise. When the surrey pulled up before his hotel, a tall, reedy man with a pockmarked face stepped away from the covered veranda. He doffed his hat to the woman in the surrey and nodded courteously to the officer, who clambered out of the surrey and tied the reins to the hitching rack. But Aaron Wilkerson's eyes were still on the young woman, taking in the dark green eyes and full lips gracing the oval face. Then, for some unexplained reason, she lifted her eyes to Aaron's window. In them was a certain calculating boldness. He simply stared back, unable or unwilling to lift his gaze from hers—and was that a quick smile she cast up at him?

Despite the nagging headache, Aaron stayed there as the woman disembarked to go ahead of the others into the hotel. Consulting his watch, he said to himself, "Almost noon; perhaps they intend to dine here." And with that he turned to the dresser to brush his thick, sandy hair and adjust his tie. Reaching to the bed for his hat, he hurried out of his room.

His appearance on the winding staircase brought a smile from the hotel clerk, who exclaimed, "Ah, here's Mr. Wilkerson now."

To Aaron's surprise, the man who had met the carriage crossed toward the staircase, saying pleasantly, "About time we got together, Aaron. I'm Desmond Kirby." He held out a squarish, rawboned hand.

"It has been a rather lengthy wait," Aaron responded, thinking that Desmond Kirby's smile held a trace of controlled malice.

"The way it is in my business."

"And that is?"

"At the moment, land speculation," he said quietly. "The captain and his daughter are waiting for us in the dining room."

"By the way, Mr. Kirby, how did you know I was here at the Western Hotel?"

"Some of my associates were keeping an eye on you."

"That doesn't set well with me, sir."

Again that malicious smile. "Simply stated, one protects his interests out here."

"As a lawyer, I can understand your reasoning. May I hazard a guess?"

"By all means."

"That officer is stationed at Fort Assinniboine."

"Your Uncle Josh said you were a bright young man. Someone we can trust."

A cold smile touched Aaron's eyes. There was the natty black suit, the flat-crowned hat tipped rakishly over Desmond Kirby's right eye, the white shirt and flash of red vest—all the trappings of a western businessman. The highheeled boots, he couldn't help noticing, were of a leather he hadn't seen before, probably bullhide. The land speculator had a cocky way of holding his head, and an elegant grace that gave Aaron a sense of unease, of uncertainty. Perhaps it was Kirby's smile that aroused these feelings in him, or the steady gaze to the gray eyes. He could well understand how Secretary Josh Tremont could place his confidence in someone like Desmond Kirby. For himself—well, Aaron knew that he was only a five-dollar chip in a damned big game, and somewhat expendable.

"One word of caution, Aaron," Kirby said softly. "It is imperative that you speak to no one about the plans for Fort Assinniboine."

"I thought that was public knowledge."

"Eventually it will be. Well, shall we join the Griffins."

Much to Aaron's disappointment, only Captain Morley Griffin occupied a corner table in the hotel dining room. "Wilkerson, you say," the captain said curtly. "Yes, the new agent over at Fort Belknap. Not an enviable job, to say the least." He reclaimed his chair as the others sat down at the round table.

"You can talk freely in front of Aaron, Captain."

"As you say, Mr. Kirby. I gave my daughter some money; told her to go shopping. She mustn't know of my involvement in this."

"She won't hear it from us," Desmond Kirby reassured him. "So far, Captain Griffin, you haven't given us much to go on."

"Right now, Kirby," he said testily, "we're harboring some half-bloods out at the fort. Complicating matters was General Sheridan's presence at Fort Assinniboine when they blundered in. Eventually the fort will be abandoned, so to speak. Just before leaving, I was shown a telegram sent by Lieutenant Pershing to the effect that a band of Chippewa are heading out to Assinniboine."

"Could be that bunch we passed earlier this week," said Aaron.

"Anyway," the captain went on, as a waitress arrived with his dinner, "it's my opinion that troops will be retained at Fort Assinniboine until this damned Indian problem is cleared up. From the way the army drags its feet, this could take months."

"This could work in our favor, gentlemen. Sooner or later these Indians will go back to stealing horses . . . and you know how local ranchers feel about that. Now, about this talk of making Fort Assinniboine an Indian reservation . . ."

"Don't worry, Kirby, I'll keep you informed as to our involvement in something of that nature. If it was me, damnit, I'd arrest all of these half-bloods and Indians and escort them back into Canada."

"You know, Captain Griffin, that the Canadian government doesn't want these troublemakers back."

"What we need is an incident."

"I'm listening."

"A few stolen horses won't tip the odds in our favor. Something more drastic has to be done. Something right up your alley, Kirby."

Desmond Kirby's face hardened as he said coldly, "Anything I may do becomes your burden too, my dear Captain. Things are beginning to stir. I've found that an impatient man doesn't always come out ahead. There's too much at stake here."

"Yes," Captain Griffin said sullenly. "Over two hundred thousand acres of prime grazing land, not counting a mountain or two. One thing bothers me, Kirby."

"And that is?"

"Why your contact in Washington would send out someone as inexperienced as Mr. Wilkerson."

"For one thing, Mr. Wilkerson is a lawyer."

"That being the case, why did you become an Indian agent?"

Aaron's probing eyes took in both of his table companions. "As Mr. Kirby just said, there's a lot of money to be made out of this. That is, if things are handled properly. Knowing what we can do legally will save us a lot of headaches."

"Captain, are you satisfied?"

"What choice do I have? Just make certain, Mr. Kirby, that I receive the rest of my money."

"It'll be forthcoming. Yes, Miss Griffin, you're back." Desmond Kirby rose and pulled another chair away from the table. As Sallie Griffin settled down, she smiled across the table at Aaron.

"Where have I seen you before?"

He could feel a pleasant tingle spreading across his face, and stammered, "I . . . I don't believe we've met."

"Sallie, this is Aaron Wilkerson, the new Indian agent over at Fort Belknap."

"Aren't you rather young for a job like that, Mr. Wilkerson?"

"At least I'm not getting any younger. I suppose it'll be a challenge."

"And did you bring Mrs. Wilkerson along?"

"Really, Sallie," cut in Captain Griffin, "I don't think Wilkerson cares to discuss his private life. I've decided to stay overnight. Well, gentlemen, I believe that concludes our business for the moment. You will keep in touch, Mr. Kirby?"

"More often than you think," he said vaguely as everyone rose. "A pleasure seeing you again, Miss Griffin." Though Desmond Kirby watched the captain hurry his daughter away, she had a lingering glance only for Aaron Wilkerson, and he added, "A well-endowed package."

"Ah . . . yes, she is," Aaron said hesitantly, the word bringing to his mind the time when a man had come to pick up a parcel at Old Capital Prison. And the fact that he could be taken back there if this scheme of Uncle Josh's didn't work out. Sallie Griffin was bold with her words and eyes, a seductive charmer. If circumstances permitted, he had every intention of seeing her again.

"Now that the belligerent Captain Griffin has taken his leave, there's one more thing to discuss." With Kirby taking the lead, they moved out into the lobby and found a quiet alcove. "Your legal expertise will come in handy, Aaron, as will my intimate knowledge of illegal activities. The captain may be right in that we have to provoke an incident. That's something I'll handle if it comes to that. So, when do you leave for the agency?"

"Another day or two."

"You seem reluctant to head over there."

"All I've ever known are the cigar store Indians."

"That'll all change, and in one helluva hurry. Bear in mind also, Mr. Wilkerson, that this venture could take a lot of time, perhaps carry over until next year. But with the stakes involved in this, I'm in no hurry. I couldn't help noticing that the captain's daughter seemed taken with you. It would help if you could

70

cultivate this . . . perhaps go over to Fort Assinniboine from time to time and call upon the young lady."

"Meaning that'll give me an opportunity to discuss our little venture with her father."

"Captain Griffin worries me."

"He is kind of surly."

"Only the three of us . . . and, of course, your Uncle Josh . . . know about this little arrangement. Should the captain decide to pull out, it'll leave me no option other than to take him out."

"Murder?"

"I'd call it a mercy killing. I'll be in touch." Flicking a finger to the brim of his hat, Desmond Kirby went away.

There, pondered Aaron Wilkerson, goes a very dangerous man. But it seems that Secretary Josh Tremont has every confidence in Mr. Kirby. Aaron left the hotel and crossed to the High Sky saloon. At the bar he ordered a shot of corn whiskey and a beer, then passed a pool table and settled down at a table by the front window.

He thought, This is a high-stakes game. But do I want to be one of the players? Despite the considerable influence of Josh Tremont, his uncle was back east. So it would be Desmond Kirby ramrodding things out here. How casually the man had spoken of murdering Captain Morley Griffin. Out here, he was finding out—especially after that poker game last night—a man went around armed or suffered the consequences. As for his taking over as Indian agent, he was expected to be the liaison between Secretary Tremont and Kirby. Perhaps this could work to his advantage.

Glancing casually out the window, Aaron chanced to see Sallie Griffin entering the Western Hotel. Forgotten, at least for the moment, was his reason for seeking out this bar and a few comforting drinks. Looking at his watch, he discovered to his surprise that it was almost four o'clock; hunger pangs were gnawing at him. Yes, the Griffins were staying over, fortunately, at his hotel. His remembrance of Sallie Griffin's promising smile brought Aaron to his feet and out of the saloon.

In his room, Aaron began removing his outer garments. He had just stripped to his waist when someone rapped at the door. Must be Mr. Kirby. With a wondering grimace, he stepped over and opened the door.

"Good afternoon, Mr. Wilkerson."

"Uh, yes, I . . . Miss Griffin?"

"Since my father has gotten involved in a poker game, perhaps we could have supper together?"

"Yes . . . yes, that would be fine."

"I see there is no Mrs. Wilkerson."

"Never h-has been," he stammered.

Sallie Griffin's eyes dropped to his naked chest; then through a smile she murmured, "I'll be waiting in the lobby—say, around seven?" To the rustling of satin, she hurried down the hallway.

He was in the lobby well before the appointed hour, wearing a trim gray suit. His anxious manner drew a few curious glances from the desk clerk and an elderly couple seated by the staircase on a wide settee.

When Sallie Griffin finally put in an appearance on the staircase, Aaron rose clumsily and crossed to her. "I hardly expected you to come up to my room," he whispered.

"Was I too shocking, Mr. Wilkerson?"

"Not at all. As a matter of fact, Miss Griffin, I found it rather refreshing. We could dine here?"

"There is another place, Delancy's; they serve exquisite food."

"As you wish." As he put on his hat, Sallie Griffin slipped her arm through his, and they left the hotel.

At her murmured instructions, they went upstreet under a lowering sun filtering golden light through fringing clouds. They crossed an intersection to step onto boardwalk again as Sallie Griffin said, "My father hasn't told me too much about his involvement with Mr. Kirby. There's something about the man that . . . frightens me. And believe me, Mr. Wilkerson, I'm no shrinking lily."

"I hardly know the man, Miss Griffin. Or perhaps I could call you Sallie . . ."

"Aaron; isn't that a biblical name?"

"My father was a Baptist minister. He died a few years back . . . my mother before that."

"Just what is your involvement in whatever's going on, Aaron?"

"I . . . well, I looked up Mr. Kirby as a favor to a friend back east. Just to extend greetings and so on. Tomorrow or the next day I'll be leaving to take over as Indian agent." He could sense from the studied look in Sallie Griffin's eyes that she felt he was lying.

And then they were entering Delancy's.

SIX

Aaron Wilkerson let his gelding pull the buggy to where the road curled around the lower reaches of a hillock before reining in. Before him the prairie seemed to be empty of life except for a couple of mallards winging overhead. It was unseasonably hot, and Aaron sipped from his canteen. For the first time in his life, he mused, he was alone and, in a way, it gave him a comforting feeling.

Things hadn't gone all that well with Sallie Griffin.

"Perhaps a bit headstrong," Aaron said pensively. And awfully defensive about her father, Captain Morley Griffin. Which meant she was blinded to a lot of the captain's faults. Definitely, he wanted to see her again. But when they'd parted, in the lobby of the Western Hotel, there had been a questioning glimmer in her eyes.

"Shouldn't be too far to the agency." Once he got there, Aaron knew there would be a message from Secretary Josh Tremont, a message sent along as part of the official agency mail from Washington City.

Right now, the sun hovered directly above him, and Aaron removed his hat while pulling out his checkered handkerchief. He was wiping the film of dust and sweat from his face when suddenly the gelding whickered and took a step ahead. With an uneasy intake of summery air, Aaron Wilkerson watched as a horseman jogged into view on the road. Behind the rider came three others, all garbed in weathered Stetsons and cowboy regalia. When the man out front reined up, his companions did likewise, to settle probing eyes on the man in the buggy.

A couple of minutes later, or so it seemed to Aaron, the man out front said in a cutting baritone voice, "You've got all the earmarks of a peddler."

"Sir," Aaron said nervously, "I'm on my way to Fort Belknap."

"You peddling whiskey?"

"I'm the new Indian agent there."

John McCall, the owner of the Warbonnet Cattle Company, tipped his hat back to expose graying brown hair. "So it's true that Agent Brown cut out of there." McCall introduced himself, and canted his head to the southeast. "My spread's out thataway. Reason we're here is that some thievin' Indians stole some cattle. Figured they were from the agency at first. But their trail pointed to the west."

"I . . . I did see a band of Indians heading that way about a week ago."

"If so, they sure as hell wasn't Atsina or Sioux. Must be those who've been driven out of Canada.

You look awful damned young to be an Indian agent."

"Perhaps."

"And I earmark you as being a New Yorker." John McCall lowered the brim of his hat. "You'll have tough sledding out here."

"I'm Aaron Wilkerson. And you're right, Mr. McCall. It won't be easy."

"Expect you'll be buying beef from me, Wilkerson."

"Then I'll see you again. Just how far is it to the agency?"

"Follow this road; you can't miss it." The look in John McCall's eyes dismissed the young Indian agent as he spurred on.

Some time later, McCall glanced at one of his men, a Texan known only as Jingles Bob. "Suppose I should have told that New Yorker about one of his Indians being killed . . . and that U.S. marshal waiting to see him—Chapman. But it isn't my way to meddle."

Another reason for the cattleman's journey to Havre was a land speculator's arrival at the War-bonnet a couple of weeks ago. McCall had told Desmond Kirby he was always interested in buying more land. Land, to John McCall, meant surviving, out here, for you could only graze so many cattle on a section of prairieland. Since most of the land around his ranch was owned by other ranchers, John McCall couldn't help thinking that the land in question was westward—government land making up Fort Assinniboine Military Reservation. Land that had never been grazed. And John McCall knew that once word

77

of this got out, the going price for this land would rise considerably. This . . . Kirby, he pondered silently, is out for all he can get. But for damned certain, Kirby isn't working alone.

Now the spire of a distant church brought his thoughts to Havre and he set the big hammerhead into a canter.

Once every six months or so, in the summer, U.S. marshal Sam Chapman would pocket a few wanteds and, with a couple of deputy marshals, trek out to the northern reaches of his bailiwick. Since taking over as U.S. marshal almost three years ago, Sam Chapman had done a creditable job. Before this, it had been a drifting life that had seen Chapman cover a lot of territory outside Montana. With the marshal's job had come respectability, a few more gray hairs nudging across his skull, and a new bossman down at Miles City, federal judge Wayland X. Zavier. Sam Chapman had been married more than once, but no longer did he think much about his only legal wife, the unsoiled dove of Ekalaka, now married to some rancher, or the two others whose names he could barely recollect.

Tall, long of limb, Marshal Sam Chapman's grousing to Judge Zavier that his territory was bigger than most eastern states had brought the warning that perhaps a younger man could do a more creditable job. Since good jobs were scarcer than hen's teeth in these parts, and since Sam Chapman liked to strut around Miles City with that shiny badge pinned to his vest, he had backed off, though his talk with Judge Zavier had resulted in two more deputy marshals being taken on.

Now, here he was, Marshal Sam Chapman, back along the Milk River for the second time this summer. All because of a telegram sent down to Miles City by those running the Indian agency at Fort Belknap. The wire had spoken of an Indian being killed, and there had been considerable mention of Indians fleeing out of Canada. Whereupon Judge Wayland X. Zavier had ordered Sam up here.

Sam Chapman said as he rode out of Miles City, "Chasing up those Indians is a job for the U.S. Army!"

"But murder's ours," Deputy Marshal Kiley Glover had countered.

On their arrival at the Fort Belknap Indian Agency, the lawmen had been told that the new agent was expected any day now. Chapman had found the agency to be a cluster of old but serviceable buildings. A few Indians had their tepees close by, and there were several corrals, but these stood empty except for one holding two mules and several seedy-looking broncs. There was also a sutler's store, which was run by the agency and catered to the Indians or the few white men bold enough to venture in here.

The Indian murdered had been an Atsina. During his investigation Chapman was told by one of the clerks running the agency that Gros Ventre of the Prairie was the more common name given the Atsina Indians. Through an interpreter, Marshal Chapman was told of how a mixed band of Cree and Blackfoot had showed up seeking food and shelter. While they were there, some Cree had stolen over at night and tried to make off with some Atsina horses. It was then that the murder had taken place, with the interlopers leaving during the night.

"Cut and dried."

"Appears so, Sam," commented Joe McVay.

"Now all we have to do is find a Cree with two fingers missing on his right hand."

"And those stolen horses."

At the moment, Chapman and his three deputies were idling in the sutler's store over coffee. Along with deputies McVay and Glover, newcomer Sid Brean had been brought along. Hard times had seen Brean lose his ranch, and he had been working down at the stockyards at Miles City when the call went out for new deputy marshals. Though in his late thirties, Sid Brean had a look about him that Marshal Chapman liked, as well as the fact that Brean wasn't married. Neither were the other deputies, for they lived an uncertain life and were often gone for long days at a spell.

Canting his head toward the counter, Sam Chapman said to the horsefaced clerk, "I would sure admire some whiskey being poured into this coffee . . . just to kill its bad taste."

"Java ain't that bad, Sam."

"This waiting for the new agent to show is wearing me down."

"But, like you said, Marshal Chapman," Brean spoke up, "the only place those Indians were likely to head is over to Fort Assinniboine or up to the Blackfoot agency."

"In any case, we'll pull out this afternoon. Can't be over twenty miles to Havre—and maybe a hot bath and some clean sheets." Sam Chapman scratched at his shirtfront. "Just being amongst these Indians makes me think of ticks and lice more than anything else."

Joe McVay, a cautious man in his early thirties, swiveled his eyes to the open doorway and held there; then McVay murmured, "Sounds like a wagon's coming in."

Rising, the lawmen trooped out onto the shaded porch as the buggy bearing Aaron Wilkerson swung around a supply shed and came uncertainly toward the store. Then it veered toward a larger building before which a flag fluttered atop the wooden pole. Handing his cup to Glover, Marshal Chapman sauntered over as one of the clerks hurried out of the agency administration building.

Aaron Wilkerson said tiredly, "I trust this is Fort Belknap . . . the agency?"

"That it is, sir."

Aaron said, "I'm the new agent."

"Berryman, sir." He stuck out an uncertain hand. "I'm sorry to say, Mr. Wilkerson, that the agent, Brady, left several days ago. But we've managed."

"The agency; a rather barren place."

"One gets used to it."

As if divining somehow that the new agent had arrived, Atsina and Sioux began emerging from their huts and tepees. These were but a small part of the Indians scattered around the reservation. In the distance, Aaron Wilkerson could see small garden plots and vain attempts by the Indians at putting up log or sod houses. Indians shuffled silently over the barren ground around the scattering of agency

81

buildings. To Aaron's surprise, they seemed as dark of skin as Negroes, but shorter and more stolid of body and face. The second thing Aaron noticed was the marshal's badge pinned to the vest of the tall man stepping toward his buggy.

The clerk exclaimed hastily, "Sir—Mr. Wilkerson —this lawman is here because . . . a . . . there was a murder."

"That's right," agreed Chapman. "One of the Atsina."

"At . . . sina?"

"An Indian brave . . . one of yours, Mr. Wilkerson. Name's Sam Chapman." He made no attempt to shake hands.

"I . . . see." Aaron looked to the clerk for help.

"Before we get into that, sir, I suggest you extend your greetings to the Atsina and Sioux."

"Why, I've no idea of what to say . . ." Detailed in the papers given Aaron Wilkerson had been a clear definition of the duties of an Indian agent, and he tried recalling now what he'd read. Chiefly, what came to mind was that as their overseer his main responsibility was to see that food and clothing were handed out to his charges.

"I must tell you that Mr. Brady treated these people badly. Mr. Brady sold for profit to white traders clothing and other staples intended for these people. Now, with this murder—well, Mr. Wilkerson, your charges are in a hostile mood. There has been talk by the Sioux of perhaps leaving the reservation. They are most warlike, sir."

"If I may add something . . ." When the new agent and the clerk looked at him, Chapman went on with,

82

"Reckon you'd best tell them first off, Wilkerson, that things will change for the better. Then I'd have your clerks begin handing out food staples . . . and for damned sure get some cattle in here and give them to these people pronto."

"Cattle?" There was a lifting of brows. "I chanced to pass a rancher on the main road. McCall his name was."

"Owns the Warbonnet. Say anything interesting?"

"As a matter of fact, he did, Marshal Chapman. Seems some of his cattle were stolen by . . . Cree, I believe."

"Could be the same bunch came in here. Well, you've got quite an audience, Wilkerson. If I was you I'd hop up on that buggy and do some spellbindin' . . . 'cause, Lord knows, you'll need that and a lot more to convince these people. And they're that, Wilkerson—people who've lost a great deal to the white men. I expect you could start off with the fact that beef'll be arriving tomorrow or the next day . . . play it by ear from there." Chapman swung over and found shade alongside the administration building.

The clerk, a rather plump and balding man, said hesitantly to the question in Aaron's eyes, "The marshal's right."

"But . . . I don't speak their language."

"Some of them understand our language well enough to tell the others what you're saying."

It was at this moment, as Aaron Wilkerson clambered into the buggy, that he had a strong desire to be back at Old Capital Prison. Or back facing a courtroom full of white people. Because, confronting him, was a definitely hostile audience. Nervously he took in the unyielding eyes in the unreadable faces, could almost feel tangibly the hatred, and even the contempt, the Atsina and Sioux were casting at him. By rights, he mused, Secretary Josh Tremont should be here addressing these Indians. Impulsively he shucked out of his coat and dropped it on the buggy seat.

"I came from back east to be your new agent."

No spear or arrow floated toward him at his first words, and somewhat hesitantly he went on, "I have been told that the other agent, Brady, did not treat the Atsina and Sioux fairly. This will change immediately. I have . . . I have instructed my clerk, Mr. Miller, to begin handing out food and clothing. But this, I can assure you, will be only the beginning. I have ordered that cattle be brought here and given to you, the Atsina and Sioux. I want to have a meeting sometime this week with the tribal leaders. Then we will resolve our differences."

Marshal Sam Chapman came around the buggy and said loudly, "Now that your new agent is here, I will leave to find the Cree who murdered one of your braves. But when I find this Cree, he must be tried in a white man's court of law."

A Sioux wrapped in a blanket took a step forward. He said in broken English, "I have heard of you, Chapman. That you are a man of your word. Yes, Chapman, you will find this Cree. Better for him that you do, instead of the Sioux. As for you, agent, there is much bitterness among my people . . . and the Atsina. You are young . . . ignorant, perhaps. We are a people asking only for our dignity and a place to live out our days in peace. This I can tell you, agent—

you will be tested."

As the Sioux brave finished his speech, all of the Indians began moving toward one of the storage sheds where agency clerks were waiting. Along with the new agent, the other clerk and Marshal Chapman went into a small office in the large administration building. When the clerk left, Marshal Chapman closed the door and scrutinized the new Indian agent.

"You have the look of an educated man, Mr. Wilkerson. But, for all practical purposes, what these Indians need is someone used to their ways. Just what the hell do you know about these people or being an agent?"

"Absolutely nothing."

"That was the first honest statement I've heard in a long time."

"But I'll learn . . . about these Indians . . . and myself, I'm hoping."

"Oh, you'll learn, all right. That you're a long way from civilization. That Washington doesn't give a damn about these people, if the truth be known. A lot of these Indians fought against Custer . . . and they have long memories when it comes to injustices perpetrated against them. Agent Brady was lucky he got out of here with his scalp. You make a promise to these people, Wilkerson, live up to it, every damned letter of it . . . or look for the worst to happen."

"Your advice, Marshal Chapman, is not taken lightly."

"Hope so." And with that Sam Chapman said he would depart within the hour.

Alone, Aaron Wilkerson looked about the small office that would be his, and then he sought out clerk

Berryman. The clerk removed a large manila envelope from a safe and passed it over to Aaron, who commented wryly, "One thing about the government, there's always paperwork. Berryman, what do you think of the situation out here?"

"Honesty will go a long way to solving our problems."

"Brady wasn't honest?"

"A man of no substance."

Inwardly for Aaron Wilkerson there was callous laughter, for if Miller or the others employed here could be privy to his innermost thoughts, they would no doubt pull up stakes and begin seeking employment elsewhere. Still impressed on his mind were the faces of the Sioux and Atsina, the despair he'd seen in their eyes, and the hatred. Was he any better than agent Brady, coming out here not as the benefactor of these people, but as a con man of sorts? But why this stir of conscience now? Why should he care what happened to his agency? After all, the man in charge of the Bureau of Indian Affairs seemed perfectly willing not only to sell Fort Belknap Indian Agency down the river but would do the same to Fort Assinniboine purely for the sake of personal gain. In a way, it suddenly occurred to Aaron, he was a prisoner just as much as these Indians. Perhaps so, he pondered bitterly, but at least Washington City lay thousands of miles eastward. For now, as Marshal Chapman had told him, about all he could do was to learn the ropes around here. Certainly he would become an Indian agent, but in so doing, he must not put his training as a lawyer on some shelf to gather dust. Somehow he must gather evidence that he could use as a wedge against Uncle Josh. At the moment that appeared to be his only salvation. It was enough, however, to improve Aaron's somewhat subdued frame of mind.

Returning to his office, he opened the envelope with the Washington City postmark. In it, he found routine paperwork, along with another small, white, sealed envelope which he tore open.

"Aaron," he read aloud. "Good news. Starting within a month, some troops will be detached from Fort Assinniboine. This means we can expedite matters concerning our little adventure. Inform Kirby your first opportunity. As for Congress, in a roundabout way I've formed a lobby that will be working against this talk of the military reservation land being turned over to the Indians." And how clever of Uncle Josh that the missive Aaron had just read was unsigned.

Tossing the letter aside, Aaron rose from behind the desk and stepped to a window. Through the dusty panes he could see the ragged line of Indians waiting patiently, stoically, as agency clerks handed out food staples. It would be cool back east right about now, with bustling city streets and many opportunities for a young man. At least, Aaron consoled himself, he was out of prison. And at Fort Assinniboine there would be Sallie Griffin. What he needed now was to be shown his quarters, where he could open one of those bottles of brandy he'd purchased over at Havre, then to forget everything, at least for this day.

For all he had found on his first day here was murder and hatred.

SEVEN

In the estimation of Captain Morley Griffin, all of the half-bloods camped outside Fort Assinniboine should, at the very least, be escorted elsewhere. Shortly afterward, a patrol commanded by Lieutenant John Pershing had returned to announce the appearance in the very near future of some renegade Indians, Ojibwa Chippewa. General Otis summoned his officers to post headquarters during an early afternoon hour when a thundercloud had appeared toward the southeast. Any rain would be welcome, helping to settle the teeth-gritting dust and rekindle the few garden plots tended by some of the enlisted men. The air had a rough, metallic taste to it, which only served to remind John Pershing of Fort Bayard, in New Mexico, and his first duty assignment after graduating from West Point.

But Lieutenant Pershing's concern was not for New Mexico but for the words just uttered by his commanding officer. He found himself saying, "Political refugees?"

"You heard the general," said a major. "Riel and Dumont have been set free."

Political concerns and matters, Pershing knew, far outweighed army or territorial policy. What had taken place in Canada—and John Pershing had read every report that had come to Fort Assinniboine—told of a bloody uprising in which many Canadian settlers had been murdered. At the very least, he expected the Canadian government to demand that Louis Riel and his leaders be brought back in irons. Just letting Riel go served no purpose, and to John Pershing it spoke of irresponsibility. It meant to him that Canada had wiped its hands of these half-bloods and Indians once they'd been driven across the international border.

Lieutenant Pershing's military training kept his emotions in check when he was informed by Corporal Buckley that Louis Riel and other leaders had left for places unknown, with Buckley saying, "The rest of those half-bloods are pretty riled up, sir."

"I would assume so," replied Pershing, as they passed through the main gates to be confronted by a mob of half-bloods.

"What is going to happen to us?" shouted one of them.

Waving for silence, Lieutenant Pershing said, "We will do what we can for you people."

"What about Riel? Why don't you send troops after him?"

"All I know is that Riel was set free. Meaning that army policy ties my hands."

"Instead of these handouts . . . give us work, Lieutenant."

"You people are free to leave here. Possibly you'll find work up at Havre. Some of you can talk to our post traders, Broadwater and McCullough, about chopping wood in the Bear Paw mountains. They'll pay two dollars a cord." Pershing's words turned the milling group of half-bloods into small groups as they debated over what to do next.

"I doubt if there'll be any trouble, Lieutenant."

"The fight has gone out of these people. But I doubt if the Cree or Blackfoot will ever change. Perhaps because their way of life is ingrained too deeply."

"You think these Chippewa will show up?"

"We only have the word of Rocky Boy."

Most of the half-bloods were gone when the Ojibwa Chippewa straggled toward Fort Assinniboine. A detail of soldiers was there to greet Rocky Boy and his subchiefs as they passed through the main gates. Wearily, Rocky Boy swung down from his pony and gazed with some concern at Pershing and other officers. With the officers was Arikara scout Kermit Iron Horn, who said in the Chippewa language, "General Otis"—an arm gesture took in the general—"greets the Chippewa in the name of the American government."

"Tell Chief Rocky Boy that he must give up his arms . . . that no longer shall his people go on the warpath. Tell him that his braves must not steal horses or cattle. If Rocky Boy agrees to these terms, then we will give him food and clothing."

To the general, Iron Horn said curtly, "There will be trouble if you ask the Chippewa to give up their guns."

"These are my terms; tell Rocky Boy that."

Quickly Iron Horn told the Ojibwa chiefs what would be required of them, and to this he added words of his own, "The Americans have many forts like this . . . thousands of soldiers."

"I have heard that litany before," Rocky Boy said gravely.

"Unfortunately for the Chippewa, it is true."

"We come in peace and friendship, Iron Horn."

"You know of me?"

"Your deeds are known among the Cree and Ojibwa. Tell your general that the Ojibwa did not fight with the Meti, though the Canadian government accused us of this. As you can see, Iron Horn, the Ojibwa are few, surely no threat to anyone. Our guns . . . we will need some of them to go hunting. Tell your general this."

The Arikara turned and spoke to General Otis.

The general said in turn, "Perhaps the Chippewa didn't fight with Louis Riel's people. Nevertheless, Iron Horn, they must hand over their weapons. They may keep no more than five rifles."

And now, to the surprise of Iron Horn and the officers, Rocky Boy said, "General, I will consult with my people. Five rifles are so few . . . in this land strange to the Ojibwa. I will give you my answer, General, when the sun touches those trees to the west." Rocky Boy swung into the saddle and turned his pony to walk it out of the encampment without a backward look.

"A proud man," commented one of the officers.

"But I doubt if he can be trusted," said Captain Griffin.

"I think otherwise," General Otis cut in. "We'll give him until sundown, gentlemen."

"Then?"

"Either the Ojibwa will ride out of here or . . ."

"No," said Kermit Iron Horn, "Rocky Boy is an honorable man. His people need food and clothing . . . especially the women and children. Rocky Boy only seeks a place of refuge."

"It could be," John Pershing said, "that some of his braves will cut out of here and join the Cree."

"Perhaps I would do the same thing," said Iron Horn. "For it is hard to give up the old ways."

"What do you make of it?"

Staring into the gathering shadows, Kiley Glover said, "A standoff between some soldiers and Indians."

"What the marshal is getting at," said Joe McVay, "could they be Cree Indians . . ."

"Nope," said Deputy Marshal Sid Brean. "They're Chippewa."

"What makes you such an expert, Sid?"

"Worked for old Charley Hankins up northeast of here. Lots of times me or the other waddies spotted Cree or Chippewa, and Blackfoot, heading for that buffalo country around the Milk River. 'Course, that was a few summers back, when there was buffer a-plenty." With the others, he cantered his horse into

93

a hollow, coming up onto higher ground but still a quarter of a mile from the fort. "Yup, from their face markings and other gear they're Ojibwa Chippewa."

"That eases my mind somewhat," said Marshal Sam Chapman in a grumpy tone of voice. His sour frame of mind had been caused by the tongue-lashing he'd received from the sheriff at Havre. The man had kept on grousing about these renegade Indians—that unless they were placed in irons, Havre and other settlements would come under attack. This, and a newspaper being thrust against his eyeballs by a member of the Havre city council, the banner headline proclaiming that a state of war should be declared by the United States Army.

The price of being a federal lawman.

Marshal Chapman spat out the dead stub of cigar he'd been chewing on and said, "We'll bunk down at the fort."

"Them army vittles just don't cut it, Sam."

"Well, Kiley, you could go chowdown with them Injuns."

"Yeah," said Joe McVay, "as much as you hanker dog meat."

"Hoping to supper at the officers' mess," Chapman said.

"We ain't officers," snorted Kiley Glover. "An' I don't see the likes of us being invited over to rub elbows with them uppity-ups."

The lawmen brought their horses to a walk, let them pick their way through a stretch of marshy ground thick with cottontails and reeds just as a meadowlark sounded. The fort was closer, its high wooden walls a dark barrier against the dimming sky

94

above, the campfires from the Chippewa encampment revealing what was taking place outside the main gates. It told those riding in that the Indians were handing their firearms over to unmounted soldiers. But Marshal Chapman noticed also some Chippewa braves wheeling their horses away from the fort and brandishing their rifles as they galloped past the camp of the half-bloods and vanished over a hillock. Then he spotted a familiar face: Lieutenant John Pershing.

"Climb down," he told his deputies. Chapman walked his horse on and returned Pershing's wave.

"Seems you can't stay away from this place, Sam."

"Old habits are hard to break. I expect these are Chippewa."

"Out of Canada."

"That's what one of my deputies told me. You figure any Cree will be mixed up with them?"

"Since the Cree and the Ojibwa intermarry, it's entirely possible. Why do you ask?"

Marshal Chapman detailed what had happened eastward at the Fort Belknap agency. "Along with that murder"—he dropped a hand against a saddlebag—"I'm carrying paper on a few wanted men. Rustlers, mainly."

Nodding, Pershing said, "As you can see, Sam, we're confiscating some weaponry. General Otis thinks it's necessary. In my opinion, these particular Indians are no cause for concern. Their chief, Rocky Boy, states the Chippewa weren't involved with that uprising. I tend to believe him." A smile showed under the tidy mustache. "But one star carries more weight than a silver bar."

"Or a marshal's badge. In the morning, John, I'd like to take a gander at their camp . . . Just might get lucky."

"You said the Cree had two fingers missing on his right hand—the one who killed that Atsina. Perhaps one of our scouts could be of service."

"I'll take any help I can get."

"We'll get together in the morning." An upraised arm brought Sergeant Ira Murdock away from the other soldiers as Pershing pivoted. "Sergeant, will you show Marshal Chapman how to find the stables. And get these men some quarters. Sam, I'll talk to you later at the officers' club."

They walked their horses through the main gates to angle across the regimental parade ground as Sergeant Murdock said quietly, "Last time you were here, Marshal Chapman, I heard you cleaned out some of the officers."

Despite his tiredness, Sam Chapman let a smile tickle the corners of his mouth, and he felt a lifting of spirits. "Just what are you getting at, Sergeant Murdock?"

"That you cleared over three hundred dollars."

"That seems like a reasonable amount. But you're forgetting the gold watch I won from that captain . . . Griffin."

"Perchance, sir, there'll be another poker game tonight . . . once these officers find out you're back."

"I do declare, Sergeant Murdock, seems to me gambling's against army regulations."

"So's drinking, but 'most every night half the troopers and a lot of officers drink away their cares and ailments."

"Wastrels, the lot of them."

A toothy smile was thrown at Marshal Sam Chapman, and the sergeant said, "Include me in that list."

"Get to the gist of it, Murdock."

"If, as I suspect, there'll be a game, you'll need a banker."

"At last the honorable sergeant reveals his true character. And truthfully speaking, I do find myself a little short. The perils of being a man of the road, so to speak."

At the stable area, a few barked orders from Sergeant Murdock to men of lesser rank found the lawmen divested of their horses. The sergeant directed them to one of the wooden barracks and, waiting until the others had gone inside, he said to Marshal Chapman, "As I recollect, that last game didn't start until around ten o'clock."

"You're still sure there's gonna be a game."

"My aching bones never lie, Marshal. Just give me a little time to see some friends of mine about money matters. I'll know where to find you."

As he had promised, Kiley Glover vamoosed to the sutler's store once he had tidied up a bit. Shortly afterward, Lieutenant Pershing arrived at their barracks and brought the lawmen to the officers' club. The fare Chapman and his men enjoyed was roast beef and boiled potatoes. There were the general comments about the present situation involving the Cree and Chippewa, and Pershing told Sam Chapman that one of his scouts, Iron Horn, would be of help in finding the Cree with the maimed right hand.

"Those Cree could have slipped back into Canada."

"More likely they'll hide out with the Blackfoot," said Marshal Chapman, as they took their ease in the smoking room. An orderly passed around glasses of brandy. As Lieutenant Pershing began tamping tobacco into his pipe, Captain Morley Griffin made his presence known.

"Marshal, one of your men just informed me that before putting on that badge he was a horse thief."

"Yup, Captain, that he was."

"Shouldn't your deputies have dined with the enlisted men?"

Grimacing, Lieutenant Pershing said, "I invited these men over here."

"Whoa, John, let me handle this," said Sam Chapman. "Deputy McVay was just funning you, Captain, and I apologize for that. Or could it be, Captain Griffin, you're still sour over having lost to me in that poker game?"

"Hardly, Marshal. One can't always be lucky. As a matter of fact, we're playing tonight . . . at General Otis's quarters. You will join us?"

"Perhaps," said Lieutenant Pershing, "the marshal has other matters to tend to."

"Nope," said Chapman with a smile.

"Then it's settled." Captain Griffin left with a thin smile for the two men.

"The captain always this way?"

"I've seen him in a better frame of mind. Griffin's changed, grown bitter. He is senior captain here . . . but I doubt he'll be advanced in rank. By the way, Sam, are you acquainted with a man named Desmond Kirby?"

98

"Should I be?"

"Not unless you're in the land business. I ran into Captain Griffin and this man Kirby over at Havre. A chance encounter. We chatted briefly. I was left with the impression that something is going on between the two men."

"Could be that the captain is looking to buy some land out here."

Pershing exhaled tobacco smoke and said, "Perhaps that's it. Well, we mustn't keep the general waiting."

As Marshal Chapman turned to follow the lieutenant, Joe McVay angled across the room and held out a small roll of bills, saying, "This was passed to me by one of the orderlies, Sam."

Chapman smiled at the question in McVay's eyes. "Seems I have a banker. Going to play a friendly game of poker, Joe. See you later."

There was a surprised lifting of General Otis's brows when Marshal Sam Chapman appeared on the walkway of his Officers' Row house. Moving into the front hallway, he swung the door open, throwing Chapman and Lieutenant Pershing a cordial smile. A servant appeared to take their hats as the general's wife, Emilie, appeared.

"How nice to see you, John."

"As it is you, Mrs. Otis. You remember Sam Chapman?"

"Yes, the marshal."

General Otis said, "I can't believe our little poker game brought you this far north, Marshal."

"The law business did that."

"Rustlers . . . or these Indians—"

"A little of both."

"So much for this chitchat," said the general. "Those we want to fleece are waiting somewhat impatiently in the living room." With a slight limp, the general brought his guests through a wide doorway and claimed one of the chairs at a big round table. "Chapman, I believe you know everyone here."

"So you're back again," said Major Dan Crowley, a ruddy-faced Kansan.

The chair claimed by Sam Chapman was directly across the table from Captain Morley Griffin, to whom he nodded courteously. He passed a hundred dollars to the general, and received that amount in poker chips. The game would be stud or five-card draw. Although Sam's marshaling duties had kept him away from a poker table for some time, he could play these games in his sleep. Pershing was a calm, deliberate player. The general had his moments of brilliance, though at times his mind would wander. The major, Crowley, had a habit of bluffing, especially when the pots were light, meaning that when the big money appeared, he folded quietly, and only then would he partake of a drink. If there was a joker in this deck, it would be Captain Morley Griffin. He had a savage, attacking style, albeit a little reckless at times. This recklessness on Griffin's part had seen Sam Chapman come out the big winner at his last and only poker session here. In a vest pocket reposed the gold watch he'd won from the captain, with the matching gold chain Sam had purchased in

Miles City affixed. Tonight, if anybody wanted to check out the hour, that watch would be out pronto.

"Gentlemen, if you'll excuse me." Everyone glanced at Mrs. Otis. "There's plenty of coffee, sandwiches. G'night, gentlemen . . . and you, my dear." She touched her husband on the shoulder on the way to the staircase.

The general called out to her, "We'll try to keep the bellyaching down." This produced smiles around the table. "Especially you, Crowley."

"Now, General, generally I'm quiet as a church mouse. Just couldn't keep it in when I won that big pot."

"Bluffed me out with a pair of treys," the general reminded everyone. "Hardly the way to get promoted, Crowley." There was a friendly wink for Sam Chapman's benefit. "As host, I'll deal first; stud poker, gentlemen."

The ante for the first few hands was a quarter. As Sam Chapman played, some of the stiffness left fingers more accustomed to reining a horse, and a feel for the game began to come back, too. Finally he lucked out and won the seventh hand dealt, as the deal came to him again. Draw poker, he announced around one of the cigars the general had passed out. Behind them, on a side table, were bottles of whiskey and brandy, but only Captain Griffin seemed interested in going there.

"Marshal," said the general over the top of the bifocals lowered on his prominent nose, "you wouldn't be investigating what happened over at Fort Belknap . . ."

"I would, sir. So far I've got one dead Atsina . . ."

and maybe some others wanting to go on the warpath."

"As commander of this military district, the report that reached me told of a Cree being involved."

"That's about it. One of those coming out of Canada."

"No," the general said firmly, "those Indians over there won't go on the vengeance trail. They've become too civilized. Before, they had to go out and hunt for their supper; now it's handed to them courtesy of the United States government."

"Hope you're right, General Otis. You gonna ante?"

"Considering that. Yes, that, and raise a dollar."

John Pershing, as inscrutable as usual, threw in some chips and, gazing briefly at Chapman holding the undealt cards, raised to ten dollars. At this, Major Crowley folded, slid back his chair, and strode into the kitchen.

"Your raise was ten, Pershing." Captain Griffin lidded his eyes while studying the hand dealt him. "That . . . and twenty-five more, gentlemen."

With his thumb, Sam reached up and scratched at his left temple—a pondering gesture. "Getting awful steep. Never realized until this precise moment I was such a bad dealer." He had dealt himself a pair of sevens and three spades, the king, jack, ten. With a rueful smile, he threw in some chips. "Nothing ventured, nothing gained. Cards, gentlemen." Carefully he watched how many cards each player discarded, as he dealt them fresh cards. That Captain Griffin stayed pat told him he'd been a fool not to throw in his hand. Considering his cards again, he discarded the pair of sevens, dealt two more face down before him and set the deck aside. Sam knew it was the arrogance of Morley Griffin that had kept him from folding.

Said Pershing, "You have the honors, Captain."

"Yes," he said smugly. But his words were meant for U.S. marshal Sam Chapman. Forgotten at least for the moment was the glass of whiskey at his elbow, and even the presence of his commanding officer. Still eating at Morley Griffin was his loss not only of a considerable sum of money but also of a watch he'd cherished. The truth of the matter was that the captain didn't like losing, at cards or anything else. He shuffled the cards he held, while gazing at the pile of chips in the center of the table. With a smile, he picked up some of his chips and tossed them on the pile, smiling at Sam Chapman. "Another hundred, Marshal."

"That's awful steep," protested General Otis.

"Too rich for my blood," said Lieutenant Pershing, and he tossed his cards aside. But he stayed at the table as the marshal picked up the cards he'd just dealt himself and began shuffling them.

Chapman said, "An awful lot of money to be bluffing, Captain."

"Only one way to find out," Griffin said tauntingly. "If you don't have enough money to cover my bet, just trot out that gold watch you won last time we played."

"Kind of getting used to carrying it, Captain Griffin." Cupping his hands around the cards, Sam began fanning them out, slowly, with a fixed smile tugging at his lips. There was the king of spades he'd kept, now a new card—the nine of spades—next, the jack for the ten showing. He clamped down on the cigar a little more tightly as a corner of that last card began to show just a hint of black. This was getting a little risky, Sam mused. As he inched the corner out more, a black Q stared up at him, and despite the countless times he'd played before, he could feel his hands trembling slightly. Then he inhaled a puff of cigar smoke disbelieving as a small spade symbol below the Q smiled at its lucky holder. A straight flush—the first one Marshal Sam Chapman had ever dealt himself or held. Only a royal flush could best his hand.

"Marshal," the captain said impatiently, "you're holding up the game."

"Don't mean to do that. Now let me see, the bet's a hundred. Awful lot for a raise in a friendly game." Eying the few chips he had left, Sam fingered out a wad of paper money from a vest pocket. "I'll call that hundred, Captain . . . and raise you another three hundred." Casually he wristed the money onto the pile of chips.

"Three . . . hundred?"

Sam's smile widened.

With an angry grimace the general shoved his cards away.

In the eyes of Lieutenant John Pershing there was a questioning glimmer as Captain Morley Griffin responded to the marshal's smile by shoving the rest of his chips into those already anteed. "A hundred and a half," said Griffin. Pulling out paper money of his own, he thumbed away an equal amount—that, and another three hundred dollars.

"Raised me another three hundred," murmured Sam Chapman. With that last raise he knew the captain wasn't bluffing. Either the man had four of a kind or the only hand that could beat Sam's, that royal flush. He tabulated what money he had left. "Only got about two hundred fifty left . . . but there's this watch."

"That will do nicely."

"Expect it will, Captain Griffin. Bet you'll be happy to win it back. Only thing is, you gotta beat my hand."

Around them those who'd participated in this poker session held their eyes on the cards lying face down between Sam Chapman's hands resting on the tabletop. There were flashes of irritation when Sam reached up and took the cigar out of his mouth, and a sudden flare of anger that rippled across the captain's face. One thing about Marshal Chapman, he didn't like to be rushed. Though in him was still this uncertainty that maybe Morley Griffin held better cards, he wanted to relish for a few moments the best poker hand of a long lifetime at the game.

"Gents, I know everyone's anxious to see the outcome here. But, Major Crowley, supposing you'd be so kind as to pour me a glass of whiskey. And refill the captain's glass. 'Cause if you beat me, Captain, I'll drink to that."

"I'm sure you will, Chapman. Well?"

Only when Major Crowley had placed a glass of whiskey at his elbow, and brought another for Captain Griffin, did Sam turn his cards over to expose the king of spades. Quickly he fanned them out.

"By all that's holy," intoned the general.

Across the table Captain Morley Griffin still had a hard time comprehending that his pat hand of four eights had been beaten. He stared hard at the marshal's cards to make sure they were all of one suit, and that a black club wasn't mixed up in them. "That's . . . only a flush . . ."

"Straight flush, Captain. Care to show us your hand?"

Coming out of the chair, his face going ugly as he paled, Morley Griffin grabbed for the glass of whiskey and threw it at the marshal. Wordlessly he lurched aside and hurried out of the living room and the house. In the living room, it was the general who spoke first.

"My apologies, Marshal Chapman." His lips were taut and an angry line appeared beneath chiseled eyes.

"They always say lightning doesn't strike twice in the same place."

"Guess you proved them wrong on that, Sam," said Lieutenant Pershing.

"Gentlemen, I think that's enough poker for tonight. Marshal, a pleasure having you here again."

Dabbing at his face with his checkered handkerchief, Chapman replied, "Sir, the pleasure's all mine. By golly, that watch is sure hard to get rid of." His smile caused others to smile also.

Out on the front walkway, Sam Chapman fell into step with Lieutenant Pershing, who remarked thoughtfully, "Though Captain Griffin's behavior is inexcusable, Sam, what troubles me is this sudden windfall. It's no secret that Morley Griffin is in debt.

This being the tail end of the month, you'd expect him to be short of finances, same as the other officers."

"Maybe Griffin came into an inheritance—"

That provoked a smile from Pershing. "I can't help recalling the captain being acquainted with that land speculator over at Havre—Kirby. What I have to say next is privileged information, Marshal Chapman. Sometime in the very near future this fort will be abandoned. Once that happens, military reservation land, which is a considerable chunk of real estate, will be sold."

"That would probably explain Captain Griffin courting this land agent."

"Yes, Sam, it would. But there's also the possibility of Fort Assinniboine being turned into an Indian reservation. And as I said, if word that the army intends to close the fort down gets out, a lot of shady characters will be rushing in to get their slice of the pie."

A pensive look shadowed Sam Chapman's face. "The end of the Indian wars . . . settlers pouring in . . . means the day of the gun is about over. Not that I have any regrets about that, John."

"The present situation with the Chippewa and Cree is a mere interlude in the history of these western territories. But it could be explosive."

"That's why I was sent up here, gambling aside. And just between us, this present situation isn't over by a long sight."

EIGHT

Desmond Kirby recalled the first time he had worked for Secretary Josh Tremont of the Indian Department. It was down in New Mexico and, like his present situation, it involved the closing of a military post. Both of them had profited from land sold to a cartel of ranchers. Kirby had been in Salt Lake City when another summons had come from Tremont. To tell the truth, Desmond Kirby had left that Mormon city rather hurriedly. He doubted that those he'd swindled would find him up here. But those Mormons were a vengeful lot.

The key to Kirby's success in any crooked endeavor was greed. This present scam was no different. Day before yesterday he'd discussed with John McCall here in Havre just how the rancher could acquire some prime grazing land. McCall hadn't been all that interested until Desmond Kirby had casually mentioned the land would be sold below the present market price. Of course, Kirby had thrown in, there would be a finder's fee.

And today, in the Rimrock Saloon, he was huddled with another rancher, Chad Morgan, whose Montana Cattle Company ran south of Big Sand Creek to brush against the western edges of land making up Fort Assinniboine. Inquiries among the local businessmen, and the little bar talk he'd picked up, had revealed to him that rancher Morgan was shrewd and somewhat ruthless. He'd also learned the man was backed by New York money.

An old scar came down to split Chad Morgan's upper lip and to make his mustache grow crookedly. Because of this he seemed to smile only with his bottom lip. There was power in the work-toughened hands resting on the table, bulk to the shoulders and upper body. A gold ring inset with a ruby gleamed on a finger of his right hand, which had been toying with the empty shot glass. The veined nose and the whiskey rasp in Morgan's voice told his table companion that the man liked his liquor.

"Something tells me, Mr. Kirby, you don't work for the government."

"Indirectly, Mr. Morgan."

"That doesn't tell me doodly squat. This wild tale of yours that I can buy grazing land dirt-cheap don't ring true."

"Believe me, sir, I know whereof I speak."

"You're spouting the same tale as when you came out to my ranch—still hard to believe there's any truth to it."

"I received some good news just the other day, Mr. Morgan. The land in question . . ."

"I wasn't exactly hiding behind the outhouse when brains were passed out, Kirby. You can find out

110

a lot of things in bars. Such as some soldier boys wondering how long Fort Assinniboine's gonna remain open."

"Precisely," said Desmond Kirby with a smile.

"So what the hell is this finder's fee?"

"This is to help ensure that when the fort is closed down it doesn't become another Indian reservation. Certain palms in Washington City must be greased, Mr. Morgan."

"I've damn well found that out," the rancher snorted. "Just who are you working for?"

"Someone with considerable influence in these matters."

"Damn, I'd sure like to have some of that land. Got water on it, plenty of shelter. Could almost double the size of my herd."

"You must remember that this will take time."

"This summer, the next, all the same to me. I ain't going no place."

"And no one must know about this."

Shrewd eyes stared into Kirby's. "Just make certain, Mr. Kirby, you can deliver on this. I'll deposit the money in your name over at the Frontier Bank. But doublecross the Montana Cattle Company, and that money will pay for a nice funeral."

Desmond Kirby brushed the threat aside with a confident smile. "You'll not regret buying into this, Mr. Morgan. As I mentioned before, this is a sizable chunk of land. Some other ranchers are interested. But we'll keep this number to a minimum."

"Heard you talked to John McCall about this."

"I did."

"McCall's a bit cautious for my blood, a bit

standoffish. But closemouthed when it comes to money matters. Expect he's still chewing his cud over this."

"More or less. Many thanks for coming in, Mr. Morgan. I'll keep you posted on what's happening back east."

When Desmond Kirby left the saloon, it was to head for his hotel, the Clairmont House. It had been a week since Aaron Wilkerson had arrived, and by now he was expecting the new Indian agent to pay him a call. Entering the hotel, he detoured to his left and found the barroom. One of the hardcases he'd hired, Yoke Rutel, idled at a table. Rutel looked up from the game of solitaire and mumbled a greeting.

"Where's Sharky?"

"Dunno, wanderin' around, I guess."

"Find him. We're cutting out to the IX Ranch this afternoon."

"Could be we'll run into some of them Cree."

"Probably. But they won't bother us."

"There was a U.S. marshal in here. Told of how one of them Cree Indians done some killing over at Fort Belknap."

"Probably that's what is keeping Wilkerson," Kirby murmured. "Now, Yoke, put those cards aside and go hunt up Ray Sharky. Then go over and get our horses ready." He shook his head at the sulking grimace on the hardcase's wide face. There was a blankness in Yoke Rutel's eyes that told a lot about the man. He'd been hired by Kirby only because of his massive bulk, and not the Smith & Wesson at his right hip. Rutel shoved himself to his feet and the floorboards creaked as he went toward the side door.

Desmond Kirby went up to his room. It was a good three-hour ride out to the IX Ranch, and he changed into riding clothes. He had just shoved his feet into a pair of boots when someone knocked at the door. "About time they got here. It's open." But to Kirby's surprise it was Aaron Wilkerson who came hesitantly into his room.

"The clerk told me you'd gone up to your room."

"Good to see you, Aaron. Lucky you caught me, because I'm about to head out to the IX Ranch. Heard from back east?"

"Just some correspondence dealing with the agency."

"Nothing about our reasons for being here?"

"Perhaps we'll hear from my uncle later this week."

What kind of game was young Wilkerson playing? The telegram Desmond Kirby had received from Washington City told in cryptic terms about the decision of the army to transfer a few companies of cavalrymen to Fort Riley. It would be like Secretary Josh Tremont to find out just how far he could trust his nephew, meaning that Aaron Wilkerson didn't realize Tremont was in contact with both of them. Yes, a very dangerous game.

"Indeed we will, Aaron. I trust you have the situation well in hand at the agency."

"Actually there isn't much to do over at Fort Belknap, except to listen to some grievances and hand out supplies. Something my clerks can do. I'm on my way to Fort Assinniboine."

"Could Sallie Griffin have anything to do with that?"

"P-perhaps," he stammered. "Also, it would give me an opportunity to sound out her father."

Desmond Kirby selected a hat from the closet, then followed Aaron out into the hallway, where he locked the door to his room. "I trust you know there's a lot at stake here, Aaron. If handled properly, we stand to make a lot of money. Do you understand what I'm saying?"

"I believe," Aaron Wilkerson said tautly, "that my uncle told you about my being in prison. That could be my lot again if I don't do his bidding . . . and perhaps yours, Mr. Kirby. But certainly both of you must realize that out here I'm my own man. I'll give Captain Griffin your regards, sir." He left Desmond Kirby standing in the hallway.

When the wooden palisades of Fort Assinniboine were revealed to Aaron Wilkerson as he came over an elevation in the stagecoach road, some of his worry about being out here alone went away. The buggy and gelding purchased in Havre, he was beginning to realize, had been a good investment. The air seemed dryer than back east, metallic to the touch almost, the land a mysterious mixture of prairie and brooding mountains. Southeasterly a few clouds streaked the afternoon sky. Once some soldiers had passed him on their way to Havre and its gaming halls.

Another reason for coming here had been the telegram sent by General Otis. Just one sentence requesting that the agent at Fort Belknap come to discuss the Indian situation. He'd seen no reason to mention this to Desmond Kirby. The less Kirby knew about agency business the better. Or was this just Aaron's way of breaking ties with Uncle Josh to some extent? The fact that his continued cooperation with Tremont and Desmond Kirby would serve to keep him out of prison burdened his thoughts. It still wasn't clear to him why he hadn't told Kirby about troops being pulled out of Fort Assinniboine. Perhaps it was because his uncle considered him no more than a lackey, and of little importance. Let the arrogant Desmond Kirby be the devil's advocate. As for Aaron Wilkerson, did he want a bigger role in this clandestine plot of Secretary Josh Tremont's, or was he merely declaring his independence, asserting that he was tired of being pushed around?

"Consider this, Uncle Josh," he threw out with some bitterness to the gusting wind, "I could head out to Oregon . . . change my name . . . hang out my shingle there—and be damned to you." Saying that, he felt somewhat better, as his buggy rolled past the camp of the half-bloods and the tepees of Rocky Boy's people.

One of the soldiers at the main gates pointed out the headquarters building. Reining in, he saw by his watch that it was almost four. There were no soldiers at the Fort Belknap agency, and Aaron eyed with considerable interest this military bastion guarded by the Bear Paw Mountains. A sergeant was drilling a squad of buffalo soldiers on the parade ground. He clattered past them on a road fringing the large open area, and pulled up before a large building, to dismount stiffly and tie the reins to a hitching rack. With some hesitation, Aaron swung open a door and stepped down the polished corridor floor. A passing officer directed him to the office of Major Dan Crowley, the general's adjutant.

"We've been expecting you, Mr. Wilkerson. Come by stagecoach?"

"I provided my own transportation. Major, I'm not at all certain what General Otis meant by the Indian situation."

At that moment the general poked his head into Major Crowley's adjoining office, and said, "Mr. Wilkerson, it's the presence of these Chippewa here at Fort Assinniboine." He stepped around the desk and held out a hand. "Good of you to come."

"Coffee, Mr. Wilkerson?"

He glanced at the major. "If you please."

"Grab a chair," said the general, as he eased down on the edge of Major Crowley's cluttered desk. "What it boils down to is that we have an untenable situation here. As you saw for yourself, Mr. Wilkerson, just outside the fort."

"The . . . Indians camped out there?"

"The gist of it. Purely and simply, this is an army post. We are not equipped to handle both the Chippewa out there, and those half-bloods. To be perfectly honest, I've been paying for the supplies given to these people out of my own pocket. No funds have been, nor will they be, I'm afraid, authorized by division headquarters for this purpose. This is where the Indian Bureau comes into it."

"I believe I follow you, General Otis. It would be preferable that these Indians be given refuge at the agency."

"Something of that nature. How much experience

do you have in situations like this, sir?"

"Not a whole lot," Aaron said honestly, sipping at the coffee.

"Here's the rub, then." General Otis pushed up from the desk and paced to a window, with his hands folded behind his back and an eye for what was happening outside. He turned slowly and added, "Actually the final decision about this has to come from tribal leaders at the Fort Belknap agency, since that land was given to them, more or less their permanent home. I had Chief Rocky Boy in here to discuss the situation. He seemed to understand the problem. But will the Sioux and Atsina at the agency be so willing to take in the Chippewa after what happened over there?"

"Yes, after that Atsina was murdered by a Cree."

"Mr. Wilkerson, it won't be too much longer—less than a month—before winter comes pouring out of Canada. So I'm hoping you can get together with the tribal leaders over there and come to some decision."

"I'll most certainly do that, General Otis."

"My heartfelt thanks, Mr. Wilkerson. Major Crowley will take you to your quarters. Tomorrow we'll have another talk with Chief Rocky Boy."

Under starlight, Aaron Wilkerson strolled slowly, and a little apprehensively, along a gravelly path inside the large confines of Fort Assinniboine. There'd been supper at the officers' club, a few glasses of brandy afterwards, without the presence of Captain Morley Griffin. A discreet inquiry had told Aaron where the captain's house was located.

Rehashing today's events, Aaron had realized once again that Desmond Kirby was a very dangerous man. Perhaps he should have relayed to Kirby that message from his uncle about troops leaving Fort Assinniboine. But he hadn't. For reasons of pride, perhaps, or, when it came to Uncle Josh, just to put a crimp in his future plans for this fort and vast land holdings. Now, courtesy of General Otis, another problem had been dumped in his lap.

Sallie Griffin—headstrong, as he most certainly was—but of singular beauty and temperament. They hadn't parted on the best of terms, he felt. Aaron really didn't want to discuss with Captain Griffin this evening the current policy here at Fort Assinniboine involving its closing. But it was either that, as a pretext of catching a glimpse of Sallie, or going back to the officers' club and drinking the evening away.

Lamplight seeping out of the open door lighted Aaron's way up the pathway. Hesitantly he rapped on the wooden pane as he removed his hat and smoothed down his hair. A woman appeared, wiping her hands on a flowery apron, and Aaron said, "Is the captain home?"

"Captain Griffin and his daughter are taking their ease on the back patio." She pushed the screen door open. "Come, we don't want to let any of those pesty mosquitos in." She brought Aaron through the living room and a downstairs bedroom past the back door loomed up. She nodded to where Captain Griffin sat at a small table with his daughter. Turning away, she threw back at him, "Got to finish my chores and hurry on home, mister."

Shouldering outside, Aaron Wilkerson greeted the

surprised look on Sallie's face with a tentative smile, and said to both of them as the captain rose, "Sorry to barge in like this."

"So we meet again, Mr. Wilkerson," said the captain around a frown. "What brings you to Fort Assinniboine?" He gestured toward a chair.

"General Otis, mainly. He wanted me to come over and discuss the presence of those Chippewa Indians."

"Yes, they have been a nuisance around here. You remember Sallie?"

"I certainly remember Mr. Wilkerson," she put in.

"Sallie, could you ask Mrs. Johnson to bring out some brandy."

"I'll tend to that, father. Then I'll leave you two alone." The smile she cast at Aaron in passing was more a grimace than anything else, and he felt a surge of disappointment.

"Have you seen Mr. Kirby lately?"

"Today, as a matter of fact. He was heading out to some ranch."

"What do you make of him—Kirby?"

"Seems to know what he's doing."

"Desmond Kirby told me he has killed before . . . and so, probably, have those two hardcases of his. You, I was told, were sent out here by the man behind all of this. Which, Aaron, is really no concern of mine. But there are complications."

The back door closed with a light banging noise as Sallie Griffin returned bearing a tray, which she set down on the table. With a swirling of skirt and petticoats she pirouetted around and was gone, leaving, at least for Aaron, the lingering scent of jasmine. Captain Griffin poured brandy into two glasses, slid one in front of Aaron, then settled back in his cane chair and crossed one leg over another. They sipped at the brandy while taking the measure of each other.

"Complications, you said?"

"More precisely, the efforts of a Havre businessman on behalf of the Chippewa. L.K. Devlin is associated with the trading post here at the fort. In that capacity, Devlin knows the fort will be closed. Unfortunately, Devlin has considerable influence with General Otis, and with territorial representatives in Washington City. It boils down to Devlin wanting the government to turn this military reservation into a refuge for the Cree and Chippewa. Can you imagine that, Wilkerson? Here these very Indians who have plundered and murdered up in Canada are to become wards of the United States government. Damned blasphemy, I'd say."

"Does Kirby know about this?"

"Just gotten wind of it. But you can rest assured I'll tell Kirby about this at our next meeting, this weekend at Havre. Just between us"—he refilled their glasses—"and don't repeat this to anyone, Wilkerson. The presence of these Indians from Canada is deeply resented by a lot of people hereabouts. Quoting Desmond Kirby, there must be an incident."

"I'm not sure I understand, Captain Griffin—"

"Something besides those savages stealing horses or cattle."

On the face of his host was stamped plainly the contempt Griffin held for the Chippewa, and perhaps the half-bloods camped just outside the fort.

It was also plain to Aaron that his continued involvement with the captain and Desmond Kirby meant his being drawn into a murder plot, most assuredly against a lonely homestead, small ranch, or settlement. It would have to appear that Indians had committed such an act, and knowing the character of Kirby and Secretary Josh Tremont, he acknowledged that likelihood. If he became more deeply involved, any attempt on his part to go to General Otis with this information would probably see Aaron Wilkerson back in prison. He had absolutely no doubt that Josh Tremont would see to that, and deny any part of this plot.

Therefore he was trapped, by his past, in a certain future direction.

They talked for a while; then Aaron excused himself. When he left, he glanced back at Captain Morley Griffin still taking his ease on the patio, a bitter and greedy man. As he used the walkway running around to the front of the house, the voice of Sallie Griffin gave him pause.

"Aaron, please wait up." She came down the porch steps, throwing a shawl over her shoulders. In passing, she plucked a rose from one of the thorny bushes lining the walk. Her smile, when she came up to Aaron waiting under a lowhanging branch, was friendly but somewhat pensive.

"Good evening again, Miss Griffin."

"It is nice out," Sallie said, brushing the flower against her cheek. "I saw you talking to Major Crowley . . ."

"That must have been after I talked to General Otis."

121

"So that's why you're here."

"And to see your . . . Actually, Sallie, it was in the hope of seeing you that I dropped over."

That she was pleased revealed itself in her eyes. She said, "So you actually are the agent at Fort Belknap."

"Barely getting my feet wet at that job," Aaron admitted. "It's certainly different out here."

"As I have found out. It's a nice evening for a walk. Shall we?"

"Sallie, you've probably heard that the fort will be closed down."

"That rumor persists around here. Not that I won't mind leaving Fort Assinniboine. Army posts are all I've known. And army towns . . . and soldiers. I've no illusions regarding either."

"Is that why you've never married an officer?"

"Oh, Aaron, I don't know. Perhaps in a year or two. Then he has to be at least a three-star general, have lots of money, and be ready to retire and move to Paris . . . or London."

Aaron found himself joining in her laughter. "Marriage is a big step."

"You've never married." It was a statement more than a question.

"There were a few lovely young women," he admitted. "Then . . . then something happened to change my mind about getting married." That, he wanted to tell Sallie Griffin, was his being sent to prison. And if he did tell her, that would end their rather rocky friendship. "Your father seems very protective of you."

"At times Captain Griffin can be a complete bore. This worries me though, his dealing with this

Mr. Kirby."

"Just a business deal," he lied, "as I said before. Mr. Kirby buys and sells land, and out here there's certainly a lot of it. More and more settlers will come in, wanting to buy land, to start new towns or homesteads. I'm finding it's exciting just to be a part of what this territory represents."

"My father said there'd been a killing over at the agency."

"One Indian killing another."

"That's why U.S. marshal Chapman was here."

"He was also over at Fort Belknap. The moon's starting to rise."

"And so is my desire, Aaron, to venture over to the officers' club. As I recall, you were so kind as to splurge for supper over at Havre. The least I can do is buy you a drink tonight."

"Shouldn't the gentleman do the asking?"

"Giving orders is one of my failings. But that was only a request."

"Request granted." Aaron Wilkerson felt even more at ease when the lovely woman slid her arm through his.

NINE

Through the blue haze shimmering in the distance, U.S. marshal Sam Chapman focused his field glass upon a horseman ghosting beneath foothills huddling below the Rockies. The first Blackfoot wore a calico shirt, blue cloth breechclout and cloth leggings; a half dozen more Blackfoot swept into view.

"As you said, Iron Horn, they're heading into the mountains to go hunting bighorn sheep."

"Their ancestral hunting grounds."

The Arikara and the marshal were stretched bellydown on prairie grass covering a rise about a mile and a quarter east of the foothills. Four days after leaving Fort Assinniboine they had yet to sight any Cree Indians. To the south some twenty miles lay the Teton River. Since camping there last night, Sam Chapman, his deputy marshals, and the Arikara scout had been angling westerly. The days were getting cooler, and sometimes a cold and blustery wind would have them shrugging into sheepskins and wishing they were back at Miles City. Today it was a little warmer, but cloudy, with that blue haze making it harder to pick out distant objects.

"The last word we got was that some Cree passed through Loma."

"Marshal," said Iron Horn, "sooner or later we'll find them."

"But like you said, Kermit, those Cree are traveling in scattered bunches. From here north to the Canadian border is all Blackfoot country. Just a few settlements and a lot of prairie to cover."

"How far is it to Choteau?"

"No more'n five miles."

"Now that you've told me, Kermit, about how you run off with that Blackfoot woman, it could get a little risky for you over at Choteau or farther north."

"Your badge protects me, Marshal Chapman."

"Maybe so, Kermit," said Sam Chapman as he pushed to his feet, "but it won't cut any mustard with them Cree . . . or even the Blackfoot."

They found their horses. Iron Horn fell in alongside Chapman, and said, "It will be difficult to bring that Cree back alive."

"Haven't seen an outlaw yet that wanted to give up easily. But this time when I get that Cree in a cell, I'll damn well take his moccasin lacings away . . . and belt."

"I heard what happened at Miles City . . . those Sioux hanging themselves in their cells."

"Once those Sioux make up their minds about something, that's it." Sam Chapman took out his last cigar as they passed through a cloud shadow. He lifted his eyes to the mountains gnawing at the cloudy sky, with some of the peaks cloud-enshrouded.

Here it was heading into the end of August and summer was edging away. He could read sign as well as the next man, and what he had seen today and for the last couple of weeks told Sam winter would be setting in early. Too soon for his liking. Even after snow came piling in, they'd be expected to get at their chore of hunting nightriders and such. The mere thought of that crinkled up Sam's eyes, and to lift his spirits he lit the cigar.

Choteau proved to be just a wide spot in a dusty road. Sighting the random scattering of aging buildings that comprised the cowtown, Kermit Iron Horn informed his trail companions that the Blackfoot knew this spot as "Four Corners," for the Pikuni had killed four Crows here. To the north, the Arikara went on, with a sweep of an arm in that direction, was a trading post, the Old Agency, started back in the '70s by Captain Nathaniel Pope.

"Pope was clever enough to get along with the Blackfoot."

The road downsloped to give the horses easier going; then they were brought into a canter when Kiley Glover remarked, "There's some ruckus going on."

"Appears to be someone stretched out on the street and a lot of folks milling around."

"Appears there'll be more trouble if'n we don't pin on our badges." Sam fished his out and pinned it to his shirt; he quietly told his men to spread out more.

They were among the buildings lining the wide street before someone shouted a warning and brought up his rifle.

"We're lawmen!" Marshal Chapman called out.

The crowd was chiefly a scattering of townspeople, but a handful of cowpunchers were taking their ease before the only saloon. The bullet holes in the display window of the stagecoach office told the lawmen all they wanted to know. A lanky man whose weathered face was etched like worn buckskin swung his attention from the dead man lying there to Sam Chapman swinging a leg over the cantle of his double-rig saddle. Ground-hitching the reins, he lifted his hat and slapped it against his Levi's to rid it of traildust.

"You must be Chapman, out of Miles City."

"I be him. Who got himself killed?"

"The stagecoach clerk. Should have known better than to try and buck the Waverlys."

"The Waverlys, eh? Heard those wastrels had been chased out of Wyoming."

"Came tearing out of the stagecoach office dripping greenbacks and throwing lead. Linderman should have known better, but he was one stubborn Swede. The Waverlys headed north—the two brothers and another nightrider."

"Just got in some readers on those boys. What about the other one?"

"I think we winged him. Had a red beard and was maybe three, four inches shorter'n me."

"Scratching at my memory I'd say that's Petey Kindahl. You the town marshal?"

"Have been for a spell. I'm Ty Barcome."

While talking to the town marshal, Marshal Sam Chapman had been checking over possible candidates for a posse. Except for the waddies by the saloon and three or four others, the pickings were slim. This meant he would have to forget about the Cree. The more he got to thinking those Cree weren't hiding out with the Blackfoot, the more this notion set in his mind. Just the same, if Iron Horn agreed to it, he would ask the Arikara to scout out the Blackfoot settlements to the north.

"Marshal Chapman, if you want, I'll get some men together."

"There's four of us and only three of them."

"Aren't you forgetting the Arikara?" said Joe McVay.

"Got other plans for Iron Horn. Marshal Barcome, don't suppose we could replenish our saddlebags, fill our canteens."

"No problem. But every moment you waste here the farther away them killers get."

"Reason I stayed alive this long, Barcome, is that I won't rush into something I can't handle. Don't think the Waverlys didn't take that into consideration when they pulled this job. Which'll work to our advantage, since they won't be expecting federal lawmen to be this close. Awright, gents, let's water our horses and get some supplies, over at that mercantile, I reckon."

They left Sid Brean tending to their horses, and Iron Horn's, at a livery stable. Another thing that Sam Chapman had taken into account as he fell into step with Iron Horn, was that the days were getting shorter, the nights tinged with the feel of frost. Which meant these outlaws would seek shelter either at a ranch or settlement.

Sam started off by saying, "You mentioned a trading post?"

"Four miles north of here," said Iron Horn.

"Unless these nightriders are damned brazen, they'd keep on going. Kermit, I need you to keep looking for those Cree. As you said before, they scattered out of Canada. But sooner or later they'll hook up with Little Bear."

"So if we find Little Bear, Sam, we find Two Fingers."

"Yup, I'm hoping. I was also hoping the army could help out on this. But it's the old policy of not mixing in civilian affairs."

They stopped outside the mercantile as Glover and McVay swung the door open and entered, and Iron Horn framed a smile. "I will ride up to Browning. There lives the father of one of my squaws. He likes his corn whiskey; and there is another daughter."

"Just don't be getting yourself killed on account of me, Kermit."

"He will tell me much after a jug of whiskey."

"Remember, all I want you to do is get a good idea of where them Cree are. So leave Two Fingers to us lawmen or the army."

"One other thing, Chapman. To do your bidding I must have more money. To buy whiskey for my squaw's father"—a wide smile cleaved Iron Horn's coppery face—"perhaps some ribbons and beads for the daughter."

The worried gleam left Sam Chapman's eyes, and despite all that had just happened—the stagecoach being held up and their looking for the Cree—laughter rumbled from his stomach. "You remind me of me during my yonkering days. Had me some wives, too, Kermit. 'Course, now that I've aged some and am batching it, I just ignore them urges. Something you've got to learn."

Night was laying its black hand over the plains when Sam Chapman and his deputy marshals laid their eyes upon Old Agency trading post, which in fact was an extensive settlement built in accord with a solemn treaty between its owner and the Indians. The buildings were enclosed by a wooden stockade, though a few buildings were huddled close by. Since leaving Choteau, during the waning hours of the day, the clear trail of those who had held up the stagecoach office had brought them along a worn trail and to Old Agency.

"They've got greenbacks."

"And one helluva thirst."

"Not much in the way of brains."

"Place looks calm as that trout stream where I caught all them graylings."

"Kiley, you don't know the first thing about fishing."

"I do so."

"Stringy steak and hardtack is all you know."

Sighing tiredly, Sam Chapman said, "Deputy Brean, maybe we should have sent those two with Iron Horn."

A man of few words, Sid Brean stopped working the wad of tobacco nudged against his cheek and said, "For sure, they'd argue or shout themselves to death." Brean turned serious eyes to the trading post breaking the sweep of the plains. On the trail, the deputy marshals had taken turns at throwing a meal together. But once it was discovered that Sid Brean knew his way around a frying pan, that chore by common accord fell to him. It had also been proved, more than once, that deputy Sid Brean was a cool hand when it came to gunplay, but not flashy like Joe McVay. Any opinions voiced by Brean were taken seriously; what he said now got everyone's attention. "They're yonder, at the trading post—the Waverlys."

Joe McVay, a man of somewhat serious bent, said, "Got that same feeling myself." His eyes slid to Marshal Chapman, as did Brean's and Kiley Glover's.

Reaching up with a gloved hand, Sam took the cigar out of his mouth. He sat slumped in the saddle, a somewhat older man hemmed in by those of more youthful vigor. "I've got to say this, Mr. Brean. You do throw up some tasty vittles, with what we tote along. But tonight this old renegade is a-craving a little more elegance in the way of chow . . . and drinks. Looks peaceful enough, down there." He pulled out his Peacemaker and checked the loads by spinning the cylinder. "Sid, got this same notion about these shiftless wastrels being there. Getting to the gist of it, I'll ride in first."

"That's awful hoggish, Sam."

He glanced at Joe McVay. With that, Sam Chapman unpinned his marshal's badge and thrust it into a coat pocket, while the deep-chested bay he rode tossed its head impatiently. He'd come to have a deep affection for his deputy marshals, knew their faults and strong points. Being somewhat older and having experienced most of life's joys and pitfalls, he wanted Kiley and Joe and Sid to at least have the opportunity to live long enough to get hitched once or twice. Besides, better than the others, Sam Chapman could charm his way out of a lot of tough spots, meaning that he knew when to call or fold in a big-pot game. That was what they were riding into tonight—the Waverly brothers. Down in Wyoming and points farther south, the brothers had earned a big reputation for being quick on the draw and for just being cruel mean. He didn't know about the other one, Petey Kindahl. But if Kindahl hung out with the Waverlys, he had a mean streak to match theirs.

"As I said, boys, I'll take point. Just maybe those critters won't be at the trading post. If so, a good meal will set mighty fine. You know the procedure; ease in different ways." He rode on, puffing on his cigar.

From the way the stockade gate sagged open against the high log wall, Sam knew it hadn't been used for some time. He saw no horses tethered outside the trading post as he drew up cautiously. If it was me holding up that stagecoach office, he mused, there would be a lot of territory between me and this place. Perhaps the Waverlys figured the townspeople of Choteau were no threat. That was the downfall of most owlhooters—too much brazen arrogance and no thought for the future.

His eyes strayed to an open-sided blacksmith shop. The forge was still fired up and throwing out flickering light and sparks. Thrust into the burning coals was an angle iron. No smitty he knew would leave his place unattended, since all it would take would be a few sparks eating at a crossbeam to set the place on fire. Worriedly, Sam kneed the bay past the blacksmith shop. The scent of freshly cut wood came from an open shed door. He stared at a crosscut saw wedged into a log settled across a sawhorse. There was enough light coming from the smithy and spilling out of the trading post windows for him to see this, and something else. Swinging down, he poked his head into the shed, and gritted his teeth upon seeing the dead form of a man sprawled below a workbench. What about those log houses hugged around the stockade, some showing light and smoke pouring out of chimneys? Wouldn't the appearance of a rider at this time of night fetch someone outside for a looksee?

Sam Chapman was reaching a hand around the butt of his revolver and starting to turn, when the all-too-familiar sound of a rifle being levered gave him pause.

"Go for it, mister!"

"My mammy didn't raise any stupid kids." Now Sam was glad he'd pocketed his marshal's badge just before heading out of Choteau.

"You're awful damned curious."

He grunted from the impact of the rifle barrel slamming into his back, and said, "Easy, mister. I just came here to see if the smitty is done with the work I left."

"Why don't we go ask the smitty? Now just ease that little sixgun out with your left hand. That's righ; now chuck it away. And turn so's I can get a good look at you."

In turning, Sam let go of the reins and his bay shied away. Too late, he saw the rifle butt heading for his face, but in the split-second left before it slammed into his jaw, he managed to turn his head slightly and get a glimpse of a gaunt, bearded man with eyes like burning coals below a high-crowned hat. Then Sam Chapman felt bone and flesh giving, along with some of his teeth, as he staggered back against the shed wall. His legs buckled and he fell heavily to the ground. Another swat of the rifle butt struck lower this time, leaving him with the feeling that a rib or two had been caved in. But he was too busy spitting out blood and broken pieces of tooth and fighting dizziness to worry about that.

"What's your name, tough guy?"

Sam managed to gaze along the rifle barrel pointing at his face, to the inquiring eye of his ambusher perched against the back sight of the Winchester. Spitting out more blood, he said, "Own a freighting outfit over at Dutton—town just east of here. Name's Chapman. Look . . . I ain't hunting up trouble."

"Trouble is what you found, Chapman, when you rode in here." He kicked Sam's hat over and added, "Now, get up. We're going into the trading post where you can have a little chat with the smitty. Just hope you wasn't lying about having him do some work for you, Chapman."

Only by clutching at the wall and door frame was Sam able to come erect. He swung around and got a clearer look at the ambusher, noticed for the first time the reddish tint to the beard and hair poking out from under the hat, and mumbled inwardly, "Gotta be Petey Kindahl. As I thought . . . just as damned mean as the Waverlys."

Marshal Chapman found the interior of the trading post to be larger than it looked from outside.

Hanging from the rafters were pelts, mostly beaver or mink. The place had the smell of age to it, and Sam got a closer look at the counter when the prodding rifle barrel brought him past it to where another gunhand slouched in the doorway to the barroom in back.

"Who you got, Petey?"

"Some damned freighter, or so he says. Came here to see the smitty."

"That right?"

Sam spat out a painful, "Yup."

"Come on, get in there," Petey Kindahl told his prisoner, and the other gunhand stepped aside, throwing Marshal Chapman a crooked smile.

The reader Sam Chapman carried on the Waverlys said they were wanted for murder and an assortment of crimes. It also carried an old picture of the Waverly brothers, so he knew the one in the doorway had to be Billy Bob. The other brother, Huck, stood at the plank bar where he could sip at a bottle of corn whiskey while keeping an eye on three men sitting on the floor. Both of the Waverlys were stringy, wore faded clothing that hadn't been washed for some time, and carried hunting knives in their belts, as well as sidearms. Huck Waverly's greasy black hair tumbled over his shoulders. Sam guessed that all three of them had been drinking heavily from the ample supply of liquor here at the trading post. Drinking brought out all the ugliness and mean habits of some men. A look into Huck Waverly's eyes told Sam the man was primed to do something either to him or the others held captive. As the newcomer here, Sam couldn't help thinking they'd start on him first. Not that Petey Kindahl hadn't gotten in his licks.

"Look, name's Chapman, from over at Dutton. I came here to pick up some work I left with the smitty."

"Damnit, Huck, he could be one of those from Choteau."

"Captain Pope," went on Sam, "this is a helluva way to treat one of your customers."

"Got no choice," said one of those sitting on the floor.

"Shut the hell up, the both of you," Huck Waverly muttered angrily. He brought the whiskey bottle to his lips, tipped his head back and took a long drink.

A pair of coal oil lamps hanging from the rafters were pouring out more light than was needed. Adding to this were the flames licking at wood in the fieldstone fireplace. As Sam shifted his weight on the creaking floorboards, he eased a half-step closer to the wall and an openfaced cupboard. A discarded army canteen with a canvas cover and webbing sling lay on a dusty shelf next to some empty whiskey jugs. Just beyond that was the front end of the plank bar, with Huck Waverly behind it. Still lurking in the doorway was his brother, Billy Bob. And just about nudging Sam's right elbow stood the other hardcase, waving that long-barreled rifle.

Marshal Chapman knew his deputies would be moving in on foot. But he hoped they'd get here before Huck Waverly got around to questioning the smitty. If the right answers didn't come, this time it wouldn't be a rifle butt doing the work on Sam's teeth, but a round from Waverly's .36-caliber Prescott navy revolver. Sam had also taken in the three small windows along the east wall, and that, though closed, the back door was unlatched. Meaning these hardcases weren't expecting any trouble.

"Hey," someone called out drunkenly from the front, "anybody home? I'm craving some rotgut."

"Damn. Now what?" snarled Huck Waverly, and to his brother, "Get rid of that drunk."

When Billy Bob Waverly stepped out of view, Sam brought up a casual hand to his face.

"Keep them hands in sight, Chapman."

"Just want to work out this broken tooth."

A scowling Petey Kindahl lowered his rifle and said, "Try any funny stuff and you'll lose the rest of them."

This time Sam Chapman leaned back slightly as he brought up his left hand. He found the webbing sling attached to the metal canteen just as a gun sounded to shatter glass in one of the windows. Over behind the bar, Huck Waverly grunted in surprise and dropped the whiskey bottle as blood stained the front of his dirty blue shirt. Sam's reaction to this was to swing the canteen around and slam it into Kindahl's face. He followed that by kicking the rifle away, and slammed a shoulder into the hardcase to drive him against the wall. As he grabbed a hunk of greasy hair to straighten Petey Kindahl up, Sam was vaguely aware of Sid Brean busting through the back door, and Kiley Glover breaking window glass away and thrusting his gun into the barroom.

"Here, damn you!" Sam Chapman's straight right hand hit Kindahl solidly in the mouth. He hit the hardcase again as a slug scoured the wall by his head, and he saw it was Waverly, behind the bar, straining to bring his gun up for another shot.

Answering that first gunshot, Sid Brean emptied the chamber of his handgun in a ragged pattern at the front of the bar. At least two of the bullets found flesh. Waverly's gun spilled out of his nerveless fingers as he sagged.

At the front, Joe McVay had disarmed the other Waverly brother. Now he called out, "Got this one."

In the barroom an irate Marshal Chapman was doing his damnedest to dislodge all of Petey Kindahl's teeth with vicious rights, when Sid Brean caught his arm, saying, "Reckon it's over, Sam."

Blinking away his anger, he released his grip on the unconscious hardcase's mop of greasy red hair. He stood there for a moment, gazing down at Kindahl sprawled at his feet, mindful now of his aching mouth and bruised ribs, aware of the bottles of whiskey squatting along the back bar under a picture of a half-naked woman astride a white horse. He said to nobody in particular, "I need a drink."

"Drink all you want," exclaimed the owner of the trading post, Pope.

Striding over, Sam grabbed a bottle and eyed Nathaniel Pope. "I'm a U.S. marshal; this one's my deputy, Sid Brean. The one who busted your window is Glover. McVay's up front playing patty-cake with that other nightrider."

"They were going to kill us, Marshal. I . . . we, certainly owe you more than some whiskey."

Sam slumped at one of the three tables, a round,

rickety affair that tilted slightly when he draped his elbows on its top. "From what I've heard, Captain Pope, you get on right well with the Blackfoot."

"I have to, Marshal, or they would have driven me out a long time ago. Why do you ask?"

"I've been looking for some Cree—those who were involved in that fracas up in Canada."

"They didn't stop here. But, Marshal Chapman, those Cree could have passed through, most probably at night. You'll need some hot water to wash away that blood."

"That, and someplace to bunk tonight."

"We have plenty of room for you and your deputies. And there's a shed out back where you can lock up your prisoners." Anger quivered in Pope's reedy voice. "They murdered Treadway, my carpenter, in cold blood. I have enough rope on hand, Marshal, to string them up."

"Nope, I'm duty-bound to bring these scum in, much as I hate doing it."

Sam felt a little better after belting down some whiskey. He glanced at Joe McVay bringing the hardcase into the barroom. He said to Waverly, "We killed your brother. And you give us any trouble on the way back to Miles City, Waverly, so help me, I'll quarter my knife across your mangy throat and leave you for the wolves."

"I'll not forget you killing Huck thisaway," he said sullenly.

"Kiley, Sid," Chapman said disgustedly, "fasten some leg irons on Waverly and manacle that other scumbag; then get them out of my sight." Sam added sourly, "That is, if you deputies don't have any objections."

"Nope, Sam, but I was perfectly willing to ride in first."

Glowering, Marshal Sam Chapman said, "Maybe it is high time I quit nursemaiding you wastrels . . . change your diapers every time it rains. Out with them, Glover."

TEN

Five years ago Kermit Iron Horn would never have ventured through the land of the Blackfoot in the daytime. Even now, the Arikara waited with infinite patience in a draw shaded by elm and oak trees. Birds flitted through branches shining dully under a late afternoon sun, the trees shedding leaves. The draw opened onto a fork of the Marias River. Riverward a hawk swooped into the draw, caught an upcurrent of air, and soared away. Across the narrow reaches of the river lay a small Blackfoot encampment. Little Dog, the father of one of his squaws, would be there.

Iron Horn took in the tendrils of smoke rising from the lodges and tepees, the occasional appearance of a squaw or warrior. Other than this, he felt at ease, though a few miles northward lay the Blackfoot settlement of Browning. Down in the draw he couldn't see the Rockies, seemingly a stone's throw to the west. Iron Horn knew that when it got colder the camp would be moved into a sheltered place. On the way up from Choteau he had run into a couple of

Blackfoot. Nothing had come of this encounter, nor could they tell him where to find the Cree. But he knew they had lied to him. Under different circumstances he would have taken their weapons and used his knife to find out what he wanted to know. But, like so many other Blackfoot, they were reservation Indians, unhappy with the way of it now, with no thought for the future.

When the sun started to sink beneath the mountain peaks, Iron Horn sought his saddle and the river. He could have ridden in before, but there was always the possibility of his running into someone who knew him. A few Blackfoot warriors would like nothing more than to take Kermit Iron Horn's scalplock in return for his having stolen their women.

"They came willingly." He murmured that with a smile.

Though rapid, the water was shallow, and his moccasins just barely touched the brackish surface as he crossed over. He broke through some willows, went up the clay bank, and walked his big hammerhead over thinning prairie grass to find the tepee of Little Dog. He called out to the Blackfoot, "I have brought whiskey for Little Dog."

One of the aging Blackfoot's squaws snaked her head out of the tent flap, recognized the Arikara, and scowled before speaking rapidly in her native tongue. Next came the guttural voice of Little Dog welcoming his unwanted guest. Telling the squaw he would put his horse in the small pole corral, Iron Horn rode there and put the horse in the corral without taking off the saddle, though he took the precaution of removing his saddlebags and repeating rifle, a Henry. The Henry was conspicuous for being all metal from muzzle to the stock, which was worn from long use by Iron Horn. More than once it had helped him out of a tough situation. And if certain Blackfoot warriors came calling, the Henry would no doubt be helping him out again.

Iron Horn muttered to himself, "Should have quit, as I told Pershing earlier this summer. Headed into the Colorado Rockies and set up a trapline."

But earlier this summer, and in the months before, Kermit Iron Horn knew the army would be fighting Indians again, all because of that ruckus Louis Riel was making up in Canada. As a scout for the army, he received a wage, and had no real loyalty to the cavalrymen and the officers. It was just that Iron Horn had been a scout for so long, that the idea of cutting and running had a rancid taste to it. And there was Lieutenant John Pershing, about as close to a brother as a man could want, especially an Arikara. They saw eyeball to eyeball on a lot of things. Except that Pershing always kept ragging him about his vices, which Kermit Iron Horn had to admit were plenty.

The Dakota-Nebraska border campaign.

They'd been chasing a band of marauding Indians when it happened, an ambush that saw their patrol under command of Lieutenant Pershing coming under fire near Devil's Tower in southeastern Wyoming, and by a superior force. Iron Horn could remember his horse going down . . . at least two Hunkpapa Sioux trying to ride him down . . . the lieutenant, John Pershing, coolly picking off both ambushers. That had given Iron Horn enough time to leap into a saddle just vacated by a Sioux warrior, and get to shelter. Now he would follow Pershing almost anywhere.

The tipi was warm, though the chilly reception from the squaws of Little Dog brought a pleased smile to the lips of Kermit Iron Horn. He would have expected nothing less. Soft grass covered the packed-earth floor, and at the fringes of the campfire Little Dog sat among buffalo robes. From the wooden bowl he held came the pleasant aroma of hot stew. It reminded Iron Horn of how hungry he was, but first there were the presents from him, including Little Dog's bottle of corn whiskey. The old warrior's eyes widened when Iron Horn lifted this out of a saddlebag. The bolt of bright red cloth was for the squaws, and the string of beads, for Calf Robe, who watched him from the shadows. She was the youngest of Little Dog's four daughters, a nubile woman of about fifteen. He passed out what he had brought. This produced from Little Dog a command that his guest should be fed.

"You are a foolish man."

"Foolish enough to visit the father of my squaw."

"How little you value your hair, Iron Horn."

"Surely the Blackfoot cannot hate forever."

"Only those whose women you took." Little Dog smiled out of his one good eye. He could be fifty, but might be older. His graying hair hung loosely over his covered shoulders. "But, Iron Horn, you did give me two horses for my daughter."

"And a good rifle."

"A rifle that needs bullets is like a gelded horse."

Kermit Iron Horn opened the bottle, and Little

Dog held out his empty bowl and watched the whiskey lap into it. With two hands cupped around the bowl, he eased it to his mouth and took a long sip. A burp rumbled from his distended belly, and he said, "Do you still scout for the bluebellies?"

"At times. What do you hear of the Cree?"

"They come like the plague. Petty thieves, all of them."

"They were here?"

"Some drifted through . . . a week ago. I do not know where they went. Also there were some Blackfoot out of Canada. They spoke of bad trouble up there."

"Trouble caused by the Meti."

"As I thought." He held out his empty bowl. "I hope you will honor my tipi by spending the night, Iron Horn."

"Many thanks, Little Dog. The leader of the Cree—Little Bear—was he here?"

"Why do you seek the Cree?"

Probably what had happened over at Fort Belknap was common knowledge among the Blackfoot, so Iron Horn told of how an Atsina had been killed.

"A Cree with two fingers chopped off? My eyes are not what they used to be, Iron Horn. But if you seek the Cree, you must go east, probably to Cut Bank."

"I shall do that come morning." He did not look directly at Little Dog's daughter, but he was aware of her. "Or perhaps I shall rest here a day or two."

"That could be dangerous for you."

"I have more whiskey."

"Yes. I see no reason for your leaving, Iron Horn."

Much to Iron Horn's surprise, they had emptied

147

the bottle and had started on another, when his host simply slumped over and started snoring. A squaw was there to lift Little Dog's arm away from the campfire. With a disapproving frown, she tossed a buffalo robe at Iron Horn, and he went to hunker down to the left of the door flap. After a while the others had fallen asleep, and though his lids were heavy, Iron Horn kept his senses tuned to the varying camp sounds filtering into the tepee. He knew that other Blackfoot had seen him entering the tepee, and by now word had been carried to all of the lodges. If trouble came, it would be when he left in the morning, and it would be from ambush someplace along the trail. In a way, it would be a welcome diversion. And he would have no qualms about lifting the scalplock of a Blackfoot even though his squaw was one. For Kermit Iron Horn asked no quarter and gave none.

Ever since arriving he had detected in the eyes of Calf Robe an unveiled invitation, and this was the reason he kept fighting off his weariness. The realization that he had dozed off came when something satiny fluttered across his face to make his eyes spring open. He saw that the campfire had gone out, and that Calf Robe was coming to him under the warmth of his buffalo robe.

The hammerhead ridden by Iron Horn was a wary veteran of skirmishes against the Indians. Its dark brown hide had scars in it from thorny bushes; a few arrows, and once a rifle bullet, had punched into a hindquarter. More than once the hammerhead, which he called Cayuse, had balked when stealing along a draw or coulee, telling its owner that a bear or Indians were close at hand. Today Iron Horn found his horse to be in a foul mood, fighting the reins.

He had stolen out of Little Dog's lodge well before dawn, and so early that even the dogs picked up his presence only after Iron Horn was ghosting over a distant hillock. There was no stir of conscience in him at having bedded Calf Robe, but the desire was there to make her his wife, and thus give some comfort to her sister waiting back at Fort Assinniboine for him, her husband.

When the sun was barely lidding over dark prairieland, Iron Horn came upon broken land stretching fingerlike toward the Marias River. Drumming at his head, and especially his belly, was a vague feeling of discomfort caused by white man's firewater. The whiskey had been more for Little Dog than himself, and it would be at least a couple of months before the Arikara would take to the bottle again. Some of the other Arikara scouts had taken too much of a liking to drink; their graves would soon be forgotten. This was a dangerous profession, as Lieutenant Pershing had pointed out to Iron Horn once. Still, their damned whiskey could make an Arikara forget a lot.

Iron Horn was torn between skirting away from the breaks so as to make better time on his northeasterly ride toward Cut Bank and a possibility of sighting some Cree, or keeping some rugged land around just in case a few Blackfoot wanted to renew old friendships. He chose the latter.

"Cayuse, I won't like it any better than you. But

perhaps we'll come across some renegade Cree."

He knew this land with some intimacy. The breaks were a breeding ground for mule- and white-tailed deer, and elk. They were deep cuts, these breaks, extending for miles and lush with timber and underbrush. There were stories told around campfires of men who hid out here and were never seen again. Once—and it forcibly brought home to Iron Horn the truth of these stories—he had brought his Arikara scouts up here to try to find a couple of army deserters. It had been a late fall day, the wind becoming eerily still, the sky lowered with a bone-gray sheen of cloud moving resolutely to the south. Almost before they could hole up in an abandoned woodcutter's cabin close by the river, a wintry storm blotted out sunlight and what remained of the day. Four days later the sky began to clear, and the Arikara scouts dug their way out of the cabin to find that of their four horses, only two had survived the blizzard. They did not find any trace of the deserters, nor were these men ever seen again.

Toward sundown Iron Horn knew he was being followed. Although he hadn't spotted anyone along his backtrail, the hammerhead was acting up again, and he quieted it with a calming hand.

The Arikara scouts were considered outcasts by the Plains Indians. This was of little concern to Iron Horn. If captured by the Blackfoot, he would be tortured slowly, giving up an ear, an eye to a hunting knife heated over a campfire, and his testicles would be cut away. Or he would be skinned—the most horrible way of dying. When other scouts had been killed, Kermit Iron Horn had simply ridden out and killed a Blackfoot or Sioux or Gros Ventre. In every instance the various Indian tribes knew the killing had been done by Iron Horn. Though traps were set for him, the wily Arikara always seemed to be able to get away. That he was loathed and even feared by these Indians was an understatement, something that Iron Horn reveled in.

During the waning hours of the day, he began using all the tricks he knew to throw off his pursuers. Then, within the recesses of a ravine knifing toward the nearby Marias River, he made camp under a cut in the high bluff, high enough so that he could watch the floor of the ravine and the east-west approaches along the river. Before coming up here he had let the horse drink at a spring farther south along the ravine. The hammerhead nipped at brush screening his camp, and there were a few limber pines piebalding the sloping canyon wall. Standard equipment for the Arikara scouts, at Iron Horn's insistence, were field glasses. Chewing on a hunk of dried beef as he hunkered down, he focused in to the south along the ravine floor.

This was where the Blackfoot would come in. No more than three or four. Back at Fort Assinniboine, he'd discussed with Lieutenant Pershing the possibility that some bloods or even Piegens could have been involved in Riel's rebellion. For the Blackfoot were as at home in Canada as here in Montana. Iron Horn also considered that these Blackfoot were coming this way to hook up with some Cree.

When Cayuse nudged at his shoulder, Iron Horn said quietly, "Thank you for telling me we have company. Just don't whicker, Cayuse, or we'll both be in trouble."

Iron Horn raised the field glass. He could see them now, a half dozen Blackfoot, bloods, riding along as if they owned the whole damned territory. He recognized one of them, Weasel Tail. From the way they rode, Iron Horn knew they hadn't picked up his trail. And they rode purposefully, as if they had a certain destination in mind. He pondered over this. What was there along the river but a few old cabins and hiding places? They could be here to hunt elk or deer. He discarded this notion, for surely they must have flushed out plenty of game animals farther south in the breaks.

"Just maybe we've found some Cree."

Shoving the field glass in a saddlebag and buckling it, he climbed into the saddle, but held there while gazing down at the Blackfoot beginning to clear the ravine and veer eastward along the river-bank.

When he'd ridden cautiously off the ravine wall, he immediately picked up the tracks of the Blackfoot. He set Cayuse after them at a lope. Through the dusk he followed the Blackfoot, to where the river crooked northeasterly and widened. But it was dark now, and all Iron Horn could make out were a few flickering campfires someplace along the south bank of the Marias. Closer, at a distance of about a half-mile, he could pick out the few lodges, and estimated the camp to hold about thirty Cree. But he must find out if this was the camp of their chief, Little Bear. They would all be warriors, having left their squaws, children, and dogs behind in their flight out of Canada.

He left Cayuse nuzzling at prairie grass under some elm trees, for he would be going in on foot. He also left his Henry. Hidden as they were among these breaks, the Cree wouldn't have many of their number standing guard. Even so, Iron Horn had, in the past, stolen into and gotten away from encampments many times this size.

As he'd expected, only one Cree stood guard over the horses taking their ease in a pole corral, the back part of which was a ravine wall. When Iron Horn heard the unexpected lowing of cattle, he stared farther to the east, and then he made out a large bunch of cattle being held in another upthrust of land. He slipped by the horse corral, over rough ground thick with underbrush, and, closer, found the Rocking M-C brand stamped on the hindside of a few cows.

"These Cree still haven't lost their old habit of rustling cattle."

The Rocking M-C brand, as he recalled, was owned by Chad Morgan, and was more commonly referred to as the Montana Cattle Company. He remembered, also, that Chad Morgan had an uncommon hatred for Indians, which was returned with equal fervor by the Blackfoot. Now the Cree seemed to be getting in a few licks.

Turning away from the makeshift pen holding the cattle, Iron Horn picked his way warily through the underbrush, coming out behind an old cabin. Wafted by the autumn wind came the pleasant aroma of beef. He passed along the cabin wall and stood there as he got the lay of the camp. Most of the Cree were squatting around a larger campfire some thirty yards away. With them were the Blackfoot, with Weasel Tail holding everyone's attention as he rattled on in Blackfoot. Iron Horn knew most of the dialect, since the language being spoken was derived from the old Algonquian family of words used for generations. There was anger in the voice of Weasel Tail, anger not at the Cree, however, but for what had happened in Canada, and much for what the whites had done to the Indians down here.

"Weasel Tail always was a rabble-rouser," he muttered.

He could make out only one Cree subchief seated at that campfire. The one time Iron Horn had seen their war chief, Little Bear, was at a considerable distance, near the Milk River when the Cree had come down to hunt buffalo, maybe five years ago. In his mind's eye he saw a flat-nosed Cree with a downturned mouth centered in a wide face. By reputation, Little Bear had a gift with words, and a firm conviction that his Cree had been treated badly in Canada. Maybe so, but what about the settlers and soldiers the Cree had murdered there? Let the provincial government fester over that.

Kermit Iron Horn was hungry, and somewhat tired. A hunk of dried jerky didn't have the appeal of this savory beef. He gazed at a hindquarter of beef hanging on a spit over a large fire, tended by a lonely warrior hunkering half-asleep before it. Iron Horn pushed closer against the wall when a couple of warriors sauntered past. He could smell them, could make out the war markings on their dark faces. When they swung around some trees, he tailed after them, just another Indian out for a breath of night air. Now he angled toward the campfire, hooking a hand around the butt of his revolver. Unleathering it, he reversed his hold on the weapon but held it down at his side as he sauntered up behind the Indian tending the roasting beef.

His left arm snaking around the Cree's neck, Iron Horn whispered harshly, "One sound and you die, Cree. You'll live if you tell me where to find Little Bear."

The Cree strained against the restraining arm.

"That is a good way to die. Tell me quickly, or my hunting knife cuts your throat."

"Little Bear . . . he is east . . . by Big Sand River."

"I am Iron Horn, of the Arikara."

"I . . . I know of you . . ."

"There is a Cree I search for also. This Cree has lost two fingers on his right hand . . ."

"You seek Grass Bull."

"He is here?"

"I do not know, Iron . . ."

Quickly he rapped the Cree across the back of the head with his revolver butt and lowered him to the ground. Glancing around, Iron Horn saw to his satisfaction that his presence had gone unnoticed. Boldly now, he holstered his handgun, unsheathed his hunting knife, and sliced away a large section of roast beef. With this in hand, he simply swung away from the campfire and sauntered off into the darkness.

Iron Horn found the beef was hot to his hand but savory to his empty belly.

He was about halfway back to his tethered horse when a shout went up from the Cree encampment.

Still, Iron Horn didn't pick up his ambling pace. There was the darkness and the absence of dogs, and when they revived that Cree, they would find that it was their old nemesis, Kermit Iron Horn, who had paid them a nighttime visit. There would be much rattling of war shields and lances, but only that, for neither Cree nor Blackfoot would be foolhardy enough to venture out after the Arikara.

"Nice having a nasty reputation."

Finding his horse and saddle, Iron Horn found a ravine trailing southerly, as he cut another mouth-savoring piece of beef. Later, there would be time to hide his trail and then find someplace to call it a night.

Now there was the roast beef, washed down with whiskey, and a pleased smile.

ELEVEN

The tribal council at the Fort Belknap agency ruled against any Ojibwa Chippewa coming to live at the reservation. From the attitude of tribal elders, Aaron Wilkerson realized this decision was final.

Here when the decision was made was L.K. Devlin, whose interest in the Chippewa, he'd informed Aaron, was more out of sympathy than to gain profit, although Devlin was a Havre businessman.

Wilkerson decided, after some consideration, to accompany Devlin back to Havre. Sooner or later, Aaron knew, he would have to confront Desmond Kirby, something that he wasn't looking forward to doing. He could scarcely believe he'd been out here almost two months, and that summer was over. Accustomed as Aaron was becoming to the ways of the Atsina and Sioux, he still considered himself an outsider, as the Indians did. His only contact with them was hearing the few complaints, or when supplies were handed out. How ponderously slowly things happened out here, the decision from the tribal council a long time in coming, the mail happenstance instead of a daily event. On the other hand, the wind rarely gave up its yammering, and in Aaron Wilkerson was still the feeling that out here anything could happen, a feeling supported by his clerks at the agency.

The weather was blustery when Aaron reached out lightly with his whip and set the gelding into motion. His only passenger was L.K. Devlin, a man with twinkling gray eyes and handlebar mustache falling on either side of a firm mouth. Devlin's bay was tied behind the buggy. In the west a few sullen gray clouds streaked the morning sky. It had rained last night, and the road was somewhat spongy; Aaron's horse and the bay threw up muddy clumps.

"I suppose we must live with the decision of the tribal council not to help the Chippewa."

"Forcing the issue could only bring more trouble."

Devlin, nodding, said, "There is some pressure in Washington to give land to these Indians when Fort Assinniboine closes. It would be an ideal place."

"Yes, I suppose so," Aaron said evasively.

"Our representatives there agree. But persuading Congress to act on something of this nature takes a long time."

During L.K. Devlin's rather short visit at the agency, Aaron had come to realize that here was an honest man—something that, once upon a time, he himself had been. Where had all of this begun? Aaron supposed it was when he first went to Washington City and stayed for a while with Josh Tremont, one of his few relatives. More than anything, it was the power his uncle had and represented. How had he been so blind? How could a man with so much influence, a man who hobnobbed with the ultra-rich and famous, be so utterly dishonest? Once Uncle Josh had stated that if you wanted a friend in Washington City, be sure to bring your dog along. Now, he mused bitterly, he'd become Uncle Josh's lapdog, as had Desmond Kirby. The difference between them was that Kirby enjoyed what he was doing. If the truth were known, Aaron Wilkerson was beginning to dislike himself, though at Fort Assinniboine there'd been a rekindling of spirits because of Sallie Griffin's interest in him.

"What do I do?" was Aaron's silent, forlorn question.

By going along with Josh Tremont's wishes for the military reservation, he was merely keeping himself out of prison. There were worse fates than that, as he was finding out. The courage of one's convictions, for one. But first a man has to have honest convictions, to try to do the honorable thing despite the consequences.

"You look troubled, Aaron."

"Oh . . . ah, just pondering some things," he replied. "Is it true that the Canadian government wants our army to arrest the leaders of the rebellion?"

"The army had Riel, only to let him go. After talking to Rocky Boy, I've come to believe he remained out of it. There is also Little Bear, chief of the Cree, whose hands are bloodied. Mainly, Aaron, the Canadians prefer that the Cree and Ojibwa remain down here. That will cause a lot of problems if they keep wandering around. I've heard that some cattle belonging to the Montana Cattle Company

159

were stolen. Back at Fort Belknap there was one of your charges, an Atsina, being killed. Incidents like these will not stop unless, as I keep telling everyone, these Indians have their own reservation. No, Aaron, I'm afraid we're in for a long and troubling winter."

"Let's see, you want me to curry your horse and otherwise tend to its needs. How long you figure on staying?"

"There is some business I must tend to." Aaron Wilkerson reached into the back of the buggy for his valise. "Tonight, for certain. If things work out I'll probably leave tomorrow."

"You're the new Indian agent over at Fort Belknap," pondered the hostler. "So no reason to pay me now. Have a good stay here at Havre."

Coming to Havre, for Aaron, was getting to be a distasteful business. Twice in the past month he'd come over to relay correspondence sent to him by Secretary Tremont. Mostly it had detailed the difficulty Tremont's lobbyists were having back east in convincing members of Congress that Fort Assinniboine military reservation land should be sold outright to ranchers and homesteaders. There was a marked interest among Congressmen in ceding the land to the Indians.

Another factor had come into play: the departure of troops from Fort Assinniboine. Just this week another missive had arrived, in which the Bureau of Indian Affairs stated their intention of opening an office at Assinniboine. Aaron had puzzled over this. Was it Josh Tremont's intention to send someone else out to take charge of this new office? He felt Uncle Josh didn't completely trust him.

Approaching the Western Hotel, Aaron was suddenly confronted by men he knew worked for Desmond Kirby. Ray Sharky, a hardfaced southerner, said, "The boss was worried you wouldn't show up."

"I'm here," Aaron said sharply.

"My, ain't he the testy one, Yoke."

"If you don't mind, I'd like to check into the hotel." He started moving away only to have Sharky step in front of him.

"Mr. Kirby wants to see you, now."

"Very well," responded Aaron. Somewhat reluctantly he found himself being escorted back the way he'd just come, then down a side street and into one of Havre's many gaming casinos, The Rimrock. The presence of three more men in the crowded barroom drew little attention. The action at the gaming tables was heavy, and he supposed it was partly because the chillier days of fall were keeping a lot of men off the streets. Aaron, when here before, had tried his hand at the roulette wheel or blackjack. But today he was angry at the arrogant manner of these hardcases.

Yoke Rutel stopped by a poker table as Sharky motioned toward the back of the large room and said, "Back in that corner booth."

Hefting his valise, Aaron veered around some gaming tables and a chuck-a-luck wheel. At the booth, he stood looking down at Desmond Kirby for a moment. Reluctantly he obeyed Kirby's gesture to sit down. "Your hired guns need a lesson in manners."

Picking up a peppershaker, the land speculator sprinkled more pepper over his T-bone steak. Today Kirby wore a natty western suit with matching brown vest and string tie. He was hatless, and flickering in his eyes was a questioning smile. "Perhaps your coming out here was a mistake, Aaron."

"Sometimes we have little choice in certain matters."

He sliced a portion of steak away and said, "Have you eaten?"

"Get to the point, Mr. Kirby—"

"The point is, things aren't going all that well for us. Which is why the decision was made to open an office at Fort Assinniboine."

"You . . . you knew about that?" Aaron said.

"That, and much more. Why would Secretary Tremont send you out here unless you are in debt to him, for some unknown reason? However, that's none of my concern. We have gone to considerable expense up until now. Some of my—shall we say—clients, have invested in our venture, and as I do, Aaron, they expect favorable results out of this. Do I make myself clear?"

Aaron Wilkerson could feel his pulse beating a little faster as a slight feeling of unease eeled itself into his thoughts. Now he knew for dead certain that Josh Tremont had been sending communications also to Desmond Kirby. How could he have been so foolish, so damnably stupid? He should have known by now that Uncle Josh trusted few people, if any. What had Kirby said before—that it was entirely possible stern measures would have to be taken to make sure this venture didn't fail. That, of course, meant the killings would start, involving the Cree and Chippewa.

"Kirby, I'll lay my cards on the table."

"Be so bold as to do that."

"First of all, I don't hold with murder. What happened back there, at Washington City—well, it was because I was suckered into a crooked land deal. You might say I walked into it with my eyes open. All because I trusted someone."

"I expect that'll be Secretary Tremont," he said around an easy smile. "I know certain facts, Aaron. First, you'll do as you're told or"—Kirby shrugged with his hands—"you'll be shipped in irons back to Old Capital Prison. Don't look so surprised. This isn't the first time Secretary Tremont and I have been involved in this sort of thing, and I expect it won't be the last. You're a novice to the game."

"You call this a game," he said bitterly.

"The money game, Aaron. I expect by now Josh Tremont has amassed a considerable fortune. I've profited handsomely, and you can, too. Wouldn't you rather be wealthy than go back to prison . . . or worse?"

Aaron realized this was no idle threat, that Desmond Kirby would have him gunned down if he didn't go along with this. Once again he was trapped by his past. They talked some more, Kirby telling him to clear up his affairs at Fort Belknap agency and Aaron saying, "You knew all along I was to head this new office at Fort Assinniboine."

"I know many things. Are you sure you won't have a steak?"

"Somehow I've lost my appetite. Now, if you'll

163

excuse me."

When Aaron Wilkerson hurried out of the casino, the hardcases went back to Kirby's booth, one settling across from him, the other dragging a chair over. They sat there as Kirby refilled his coffee cup, a man pondering the options open to him. There was little doubt in his mind that the weak link in this was Wilkerson. Why was a man who'd been involved in criminal activities before, so reluctant now? Perhaps Wilkerson still clung to the strange notion that he had a sterling character, or it simply could be a matter of conscience. Some men were like that—those who would never make it out here. A pity, he mused, for with Wilkerson's background as a lawyer, the man could be of considerable use.

Shoving the plate away, Desmond Kirby reached for a cigar. "What have you found out, Sharky?"

"For one thing, it's getting damned cold out there. But I sounded out this half-blood, LaVallier. Like you said, Mr. Kirby, all these Indians and half-bloods have to look forward to are hard times."

"You gave LaVallier some money to help him make up his mind."

"Latched onto it mighty quick-like. Said he'd hunt up some old Cree friends of his, namely a warrior, Grass Bull."

"I'm not looking, Sharky, to start wholesale slaughter. Take out a nester here . . . a cowhand or two someplace else . . . should provoke the army into rounding up these damned renegade Indians and escorting them back to Canada."

"Just told LaVallier the bare bones of what you want done, Mr. Kirby. But according to him, a bunch

164

of Cree and Chippewa, and even some Blackfoot, have split away from their tribes. Hiding out in those breaks along the Marias River . . . and other places, I gather. Just when do you want me to get together with this half-blood again?"

"This, Mr. Sharky, is a waiting game." He told Yoke Rutel to fetch him a bottle of whiskey and three glasses. "Someone with considerable influence is backing our play. It just could be there'll be no need to use the half-blood and those Indians, but we most surely will if that becomes necessary."

TWELVE

In the afternoon mail there was a letter for Lieutenant John Pershing. The Wyoming postmark was all that the young lieutenant needed to put away the report he was preparing for General Otis about the Indian situation. With his pipe in hand, Pershing went to an orderly room window and stood there reading the letter. It spoke of winter settling upon Wyoming and asked when a certain lady could expect a visit.

Fixing his eyes on the nearby barracks and stable area, Pershing realized that Fort Assinniboine was slowly being evacuated. Only two other cavalry units and his Tenth Cavalry were still detailed here. From the reports brought in by the Arikara scouts, notably Kermit Iron Horn, the Chippewa were now encamped north of Havre. Many problems would have been solved had the Ojibwa Chippewa been allowed to stay at the Fort Belknap agency. The Cree and their Blackfoot allies were scattered farther to the northwest. More than a month ago, U.S. marshal Sam

Chapman had returned with a couple of outlaws, and was handed a telegram stating that Chapman's presence was required back at Miles City. Still roaming around out there was the Cree wanted for committing a murder at the Indian agency, some warrior named Grass Bull.

Once a week, elements of Lieutenant Pershing's command would head out to patrol the areas where these Indians were encamped. They'd bring along packhorses laden with supplies, and invariably these patrols would be accosted along the way by either a rancher or nester. It was difficult avoiding the small cowtowns where it seemed the presence of the army was resented.

Swinging away from the window, he stepped to the potbellied stove and picked up the coffeepot. "Out here, people seem to forget how the army fought the Sioux."

"Nossir, Lo'tenant," said First Sergeant Elijah Moore, another veteran of the Indian Wars. "It's not that they've forgotten those bloody days. Just don't want to think about a lot of painful memories."

"Yes, you're right, Sergeant. We've all been affected by these long conflicts."

"But for us, sir, it's the life we've chosen."

"What's the word on tomorrow's weather?"

"Cold, windy, probably some snow."

"At least we can depend on it being windy up here, and tolerably cold. The one constant we have, it seems."

"Sir, scuttlebutt has it we might be rounding up these Indians—"

"I fell it'll come down to that."

"Either that, or the ranchers are going to do some rounding up of their own. A lot of cattle have been rustled courtesy of the Cree and Chippewa. Besides, the men are getting tired of riding out for no other purpose than to be supply bearers and such."

"Perhaps what they really need are more drill formations."

"That should stop their grumbling, Lo'tenant."

With a smile for Sergeant Moore, Pershing donned his winter coat and campaign hat, pulling on a pair of gloves as he left the building. His reason for leaving was to confer with the general's adjutant, Major Dan Crowley, about the quartermaster issuing more winter clothing for his buffalo soldiers. On his way, John Pershing passed a wooden frame building that had been turned over to the Bureau of Indian Affairs. He had come to be on speaking terms with Aaron Wilkerson, but it still troubled him that another government agency had moved in before this military reservation was turned over to civilian control. A couple of times he had seen Captain Morley Griffin entering the building. Lately, as noticed by Pershing and other officers, Griffin had been more withdrawn than usual. Perhaps the captain's being bested at poker by Marshal Chapman had something to do with it. Or maybe Morley Griffin had made some unwise investments.

As he neared post headquarters, Sergeant-Major J.B. Callahan came striding outside and said, "Lieutenant, just the man I want to see. Seems a couple of cowboys got killed over in that Square Butte country."

"By rustlers?"

"The telegram we received stated they were killed by Indians. Major Crowley is waiting inside. I'm on my way over to General Otis's quarters." The sergeant hurried away.

John Pershing found the adjutant's office, and with Major Crowley were two officers from the Ninth Cavalry. The officers were clustered around a map spread out on Crowley's desk. "Pershing, glad you're here."

"I ran into Sergeant Callahan just as he left. Indians, he said?"

"According to this telegram." The major picked up the telegram and passed it to Pershing.

"Hmm. All it says is that some hostile Indians killed these men and stole some cattle. Could be Sioux or Blackfoot?"

"Could be, John. The general will be right here. But I know he'll want you to head over there and check this out."

"Over by Square Butte? That's on land owned by the Montana Cattle Company. As I recall, major, Chad Morgan has a special hatred for Indians."

"That telegram was sent by the marshal at Loma, Bill Lonigan. If Lonigan says Indians were involved in this, I have to believe him."

Footsteps resounded in the hallway, and a moment later General Otis strode in. "So, gentlemen, it has come to this."

"According to Marshal Lonigan over at Loma, sir."

"Lieutenant Pershing, you'll take a patrol out in the morning. Take all of the Arikara scouts."

"I probably should leave this afternoon."

"As you wish, John. I hope the Cree and Chippewa weren't involved in this. But in any case, gentlemen, I received a dispatch from regimental headquarters earlier today. I might as well tell you now that an agreement has been worked out between the Canadian government and ours. What it boils down to is that Canada wants us to arrest the leaders of the rebellion and escort them up to the line. Too bad that we let Louis Riel and that Dumont go. Now they want the Indian leaders—Little Bear and some of his chiefs . . . and Rocky Boy of the Chippewa. But that will have to wait, I'm afraid, while we look into this matter."

"You said Rocky Boy?"

"Yes, John, the Canadians believe he and his Chippewa joined in that uprising."

Major Crowley spoke. "Pershing and I discussed that, sir. We find that hard to believe, especially when you consider that the Chippewa brought their women and children along. As it is detailed in official dispatches, those who fought in the uprising broke across the border in scattered bunches . . . and barely a jump ahead of Canadian soldiers."

"It'll bear looking into," said General Otis. "Good luck, Lieutenant Pershing. One final word. If the Cree did this—and I pray this isn't the case—bring your report to me personally. A telegram sent from Loma could be intercepted. And then who knows what these ranchers will do."

Aaron Wilkerson was getting used to the bugle calls dominating the way of life here at Fort Assinniboine. He had fallen into the routine of coming to his office around eight o'clock to handle a few mundane chores. His seeing Sallie Griffin had been accepted grudgingly by her father.

Once in a while Captain Morley Griffin would fill Aaron in on new army policy regarding the Indians. More often, though, it would be the captain riding into Havre, he supposed to talk things over with Desmond Kirby.

Winter was getting a firm grip on the land. He had been surprised at the severity of it, how the wind never ceased its constant yammering, but mostly, for someone used to eastern seaboard weather, it was a cold that struck to the bone. At the sutler's store he'd bought new winter clothing, a mackinaw, fur cap and heavy boots.

Aaron had fallen into the routine of going for a horseback ride with Sallie every so often. At first, during Indian Summer, it had given him a contented feeling just being alone with her, with the brooding sweep of the plains, the few trees tinged with red or green or golden brown. That she spoke French came as a surprise, as did her knowledge of army ways. Sometimes, as tonight, Aaron was invited for supper. More and more the captain had begun to isolate himself, and Aaron Wilkerson was aware of Morley Griffin's unspoken disapproval of Aaron's intentions concerning his daughter.

One evening he'd gone over there and Sallie had told him the captain had gone into Havre for a weekend visit. After dismissing the housekeeper, Sallie had prepared supper. Later, on the settee in the living room, Aaron had spoken somewhat hesitantly of love and his undecided plans for the future.

"Mr. Wilkerson," she'd replied boldly, "you are most definitely the man I'm going to marry."

"I am?"

"I've known that from the first moment I set eyes on you . . . way back at Havre." She snuggled into his arms.

"I . . . Sallie, I won't always be an Indian agent."

"Nor do I want to remain at Fort Assinniboine all my life. Truthfully, my love, I've grown weary of the army. Lately"—she groped for the right words—"my father hasn't been himself. It seems every time he goes into Havre he gambles . . . and loses. Aaron, we're not all that rich."

"Perhaps the captain has grown weary of army life, too."

"I don't know what it is. Only that he's changed."

And for Aaron the temptation was there to break down and tell Sallie Griffin his true reason for being out here. This headstrong woman most certainly would not marry a former convict, a thief. Wouldn't it be better for all concerned that he simply pack up and head out—yes, head out to that Oregon country. Change his name, start over again. But when they kissed, his heart beat with an agonizing fear that his confession would end this, and he let the moment pass.

The door opening jerked Aaron's thoughts away from Sallie Griffin and to her father, Captain Morley Griffin, striding over the threshold and into his office. Without preamble the captain said, "It's begun."

"Sir?"

"The killings."

"So . . . soon?" An empty feeling pitted his stomach.

"Take a walk outside with me, Wilkerson." This was a command more than a request, and Captain Griffin swung around as Aaron shoved up from his desk.

They walked silently to get a better view of the parade grounds and troops from Lieutenant Pershing's Tenth Cavalry assembling there. In the center of the vast acreage the stars and stripes tugged at its moorings, and a cold wind beat at them.

Captain Griffin said stonily, "Cree Indians killed a couple of cowhands west of here."

"By order of . . . Desmond Kirby?"

"Of course, Wilkerson. Which means the price for my services has just gone up." He swung his eyes toward Aaron. "This could prompt the army to round these savages up and send them packing. Which, mark my words, might just happen. And another thing, Wilkerson. I want you to stop seeing my daughter."

"But . . . we're just friends . . ."

"I know about you, Wilkerson. Desmond Kirby told me the hard facts of how you were sent out here . . . and something about your less than desirable background. Nothing personal, you understand. When this is over, we'll be going back east, where my daughter can marry someone presentable."

"And you consider yourself presentable?" Aaron said bitterly.

"It doesn't matter what you think of me," he retorted. "From now on this is strictly business between us. Leave her be." Uttering those threatening words, the captain headed in the direction of the officers' club.

Now it was out in the open, he pondered—just what the captain thought of him—and in a way he couldn't blame Morley Griffin. Just what could a convicted felon offer a woman like Sallie; how could he expect to make her a part of his life? Aaron saw a very bleak future for himself. But to just stop seeing the woman he loved, especially when she was only across the wide confines of Fort Assinniboine, cut to the quick. Perhaps if he threatened to reveal Captain Griffin's part in this— Aaron quickly discarded that notion.

With some degree of envy he watched Lieutenant John Pershing bring his buffalo soldiers out of the main gates. Only now did he become aware that he was out here without a coat or hat. Shrugging, Aaron moved slowly toward his office, even as his eyes drifted northwesterly in the direction of Sallie Griffin's home.

Why did this have to happen now?

THIRTEEN

Near the end of another cold day, Lieutenant John Pershing and his buffalo soldiers rode into Loma, past the First Baptist Church to their left, with white paint peeling from its bell tower, and the cemetery rising along a snow-speckled hillock. When they wheeled onto Main Street, hard under the shod hooves of their mounts, resentful eyes took in the Negro cavalrymen commanded by a white officer.

John Pershing had grown accustomed to the prejudiced attitude of many people toward the men he commanded. Up here were many of those who had left their southern homes after the end of the Civil War, and of course a few "galvanized Yankees"—former Rebel prisoners-of-war who had been paroled out of federal prisons, then clothed in Yankee blue and sent out west to help defend western forts and the settlers against the Plains Indians. These men had settled in, gotten married, and become members of the community as surely as those who had sailed over from Europe. Some of these former southerners were tolerant toward the buffalo soldiers; still, they kept their distance.

They'd ridden hard today, would push on tomorrow and out to Square Butte. Pershing had sent the Arikara scouts on ahead; to make certain they weren't mistaken for hostiles, he had sent with them several of his cavalrymen. Glancing skyward, he frowned at the solid patches of gray cloud. There was snow on the way; he could almost smell it. Any snowfall now would wipe out the trail left by those Indians. But, as he'd said to Kermit Iron Horn, it was almost a certainty that those who'd committed murder would beeline north into Blackfoot country.

Sighting Eisenbarth's Funeral Parlor, he brought the column to a halt. To Sergeant Ira Murdock he said, "There's a spring about a half mile out of town. We'll bivouac there." John Pershing brought his horse across the street and dismounted.

The only display window in the funeral parlor was covered with thick white drapes, and no light showed through the glass in the door. The knob turned easily in his hand, however, and he went inside. To his right, in a large room barren of furniture but for a row of chairs placed along one wall, and some flowers in vases, there was an open coffin. The body in it was that of an elderly man, the white hair pasted back, the face a pale, serene color. It was Pershing's hope that the bodies of those two cowhands had been brought here for a proper burial. The door to the room opposite opened, and he turned that way.

A middle-aged man with a questioning smile gazed at Lieutenant Pershing. His eyes behind the thick glasses were a mellow brown. He reached up and brushed a fly away from his fringe of hair.

"Could I be of help, Lieutenant?"

"Mr. Eisenbarth?"

"The only employee of this humble establishment."

"We received a report that two cowhands were murdered by some renegade Indians. Were the bodies brought here, Mr. Eisenbarth?"

"Heavens no," he replied. "From what I gather, they were buried out at the ranch."

"That would be Chad Morgan's Montana Cattle Company?"

"It would, Lieutenant . . ."

"Pershing; forgive my abruptness."

"Come to think of it, Doc Skroms was called out there. Left rather hurriedly with one of Morgan's hands. As I understand, Lieutenant Pershing, one of them survived that attack, but he died before Doc Skroms could get out there."

"Where can I find Doc Skroms?"

"Downstreet, the next block."

With a smile for the undertaker, he went outside, loosened the reins from the hitching rack, and led the gelding past some locals congregated in front of a mercantile. He nodded pleasantly; their idle prattling ceased. Other townspeople had drifted out to get a gander at the buffalo soldiers, as had the town marshal, Lonigan, who stepped off the boardwalk and fell into step with Pershing. Lonigan had long, dangling arms and walked with a slight stoop, the white-thatched hair growing shaggy around his ears and neck. He wore no gun, and suspenders held up trousers patched at the right knee.

"Glad they sent you over, Lieutenant, instead of

179

that captain . . . that Griffin. Eisenbarth probably told you they buried those boys out at Morgan's place. I went out with Doc Skroms."

"What did happen?"

"These hands of Morgan's were at a line camp—you know, the one north of Square Butte. They were jumped by a bunch of Cree . . . and maybe some Blackfoot. Never had no chance. Some other waddies heard guns being fired and rode lickety-split over there, about in time to drive them Indians off."

"Did you check for sign out there?"

"When me and Doc Skroms got to the ranch, Chad Morgan said there was no need to head over there. Later, after Millard died, I took off on my lonesome out to that line shack."

Approaching a whitewashed building just past a corner saloon and set back from the street, they nodded at Doc Jan Skroms closing the door and striding up the walkway toward them. Somewhat over six feet, Doc Skroms wore a rumpled black suit and cattleman's hat and boots. He had a prominent nose centered on a long face, and was cleanshaven. He nodded courteously as the marshal introduced the lieutenant from Fort Assinniboine.

"Yes, I have heard you were here before, Lieutenant Pershing. In an official capacity, of course."

"Now it seems murder has brought me out here, sir. Do you agree with Chad Morgan, that it was renegade Cree who killed these men?"

"When we left town it was to head directly for the home ranch. There I found only the one man still alive, a Davey Millard. But despite all my efforts, he passed away that evening. No, I could not say whether Indians killed these men, Lieutenant Pershing, as they died from bullet wounds. Rustlers are also active in these parts, unfortunately."

"Morgan's hands claim it was Indians," said Marshal Lonigan.

"Did they actually see them?"

"Claimed they was too far away to be downright certain as to what tribe they were from, though it was Chad Morgan spouting off that some Cree did the killings. Him never being even close to that line shack, but back at the ranch, makes me wonder. But no question about it, they were Indians. Found their tracks coming in—other tracks running to the north. Getting dark then, and being alone, I decided to head back to Loma."

"Thank you, gentlemen, for your help." Moving to his horse, Pershing climbed into the saddle and cantered downstreet under the watchful eyes of a few locals.

What troubled John Pershing was that there'd been no mention of why those Indians were there. Not one word had been dropped about rustling cattle or horses. If they were Cree, a tribe renowned for stealing horses, it would make more sense that they would go after Chad Morgan's horse herd. To simply take out a couple of waddies at some forlorn line shack didn't ring true.

Perhaps there was an ulterior motive?

What better way to persuade the army to round up the Cree and Chippewa than to have some of them go around killing cowhands or nesters? Once the Indians were escorted back into Canada, any talk of turning Fort Assinniboine military reservation into a haven for the same Indians would be abandoned. This would simplify matters for those wanting to sell the military reservation to—say—a rancher or two, or some land speculators.

That promptly set John Pershing's mind turning to a fellow officer at Assinniboine, Captain Morley Griffin. Of course, at Havre, about a month or two ago, he'd seen Griffin engrossed in conversation with a man named Kirby. As he recalled Griffin telling him, this Kirby was some sort of land agent.

Lieutenant Pershing had passed the lane running southward to where his men were encamped, before he realized his mistake, and he swung his horse around and angled that way. Now he felt more keenly the biting cold wind moaning under the cedar and pine trees. Part of his thoughts were still probing for answers to these killings, and Captain Morley Griffin's possible involvement in something that could speak poorly for the officer corps at Fort Assinniboine.

Morley Griffin? Greedy, yes. Capable of a criminal act? Only if the stakes were high enough. Obviously they were high, very high, for murder had been committed.

Kermit Iron Horn and his Arikara scouts, and the handful of soldiers attached to the Tenth Cavalry, had ghosted past scattered bunches of grazing cattle on their way across Montana Cattle Company land. Iron Horn had sent out two scouts to ride point, ever since bypassing the cowtown of Loma late last night. He didn't want to stumble across any cowhands out here, since these men were likely to blaze away and ask any questions later.

Snow fell lazily out of a chiseled gray sky. On the rough ground old snow lay here and there, deeper in depressions and low pockets of land. Mostly they held to a canter, the wind gouging at their exposed flesh, swirling away hoarfrost from their nostrils and mouths, and from the horses they rode. Presently they were passing along a draw, strung out and looking for a place to noon. They found a place upon loping out of this draw and into a deeper one guarded by a sandstone wall marked by vari-colored stripes piled one upon the other as though there since creation. In here the sagebrush was thick, the grass of summer dying, the wind just a notion above rimrock.

A grunted command from Iron Horn brought them closing in, and out of their saddles.

Commanding the soldiers was Sergeant Luke Robeson, in his late twenties, once a young dreamer out of Georgia. Along with the others, Robeson tended to his horse first, loosening the saddle cinches before letting it graze. Among the troopers of Company H, the Tenth Cavalry, he was considered something of a learned man, an opinion he did not take lightly. For the here and now, Luke Robeson had found a home, but he burned inwardly with the idea that someday he would make his mark as a civilian. This meant gaining that college degree, as had his doctor father. But when a man had been wounded twice and still had a couple of years to serve in this hostile land, there was little room for dreams. This was the reason Sergeant Robeson had ceded command of his patrol to Iron Horn.

The campfire drew everyone within squatting distance, though the Arikara scouts lingered off to one side. As the coffeepot warmed, and the fire roasted pieces of rabbit shot earlier this morning, Iron Horn and Sergeant Robeson chatted quietly.

"Now this, after all we've been through."

"What you're getting paid to do, Robeson."

"You always did look at the grim side of things."

"My nature."

"Suppose it wasn't Indians?"

"I wouldn't mind scalping a white man, then." Kermit Iron Horn unleashed a slow smile. "But like you, Robeson, I'm more worried about cowhands with edgy trigger-fingers."

"How do you do it, Kermit? How in the hell can you help us soldier boys find your . . . brethren?"

From the pocket of his buffalo fur coat Iron Horn took out a small flask, unscrewing the cap while mulling over Robeson's question. He took a long swallow of whiskey; it was hot in his mouth and spread a glow in his belly. One eye lidded down as he took another long sip from the flask, and, wiping at his mouth with a coat sleeve, he said, "Scouting after Sioux or Gros Ventre is one and the same to me. And they ain't my brethren, Robeson. Here, warm your innards." He passed the flask over, and plucked a hunk of rabbit away from the wooden spit over the campfire.

Twenty minutes later they had stomped out the campfire and were saddlebound.

Around midafternoon, one of those who'd been out riding point, an Arikara named Charley Ten Sleep, appeared so suddenly that two of the buffalo soldiers went scrambling for their rifles. They'd barely got their weapons out of their scabbards before Sergeant Robeson's words of contempt came sidling over the quartering wind. "Damnit, you men ought to have better sense than that . . . and eyes!"

"What have you got, Charley?" inquired Iron Horn.

The scout twisted in the saddle and swept an arm toward Square Butte about two miles away, cloaked by falling snow. "They keep watch from up there."

"Fools." Iron Horn glanced at Robeson. "Only fools would expect the Cree to come back. This snow—what do you think?"

Sergeant Robeson said, "Not snowing all that much. But snow or not, Kermit, I've seen you track through worse."

He accepted the compliment with a grimace. "That creek off to our right . . . the trees lining it should shelter us until we find that line camp."

Iron Horn proved to be right, for they had encountered no Montana Cattle Company riders when an old log cabin and pole corral appeared below a bluff. They went in, then stopped a half dozen or so rods out as Iron Horn and his scouts spread out and began earning their pay. It was no more than ten minutes later that an arm signal from Iron Horn brought in Sergeant Robeson and the others.

"Indians were here, judging from all the unshod hoof markings we found. Seven of them. Rode in from the west . . . hit the line shack from both sides . . . Afterwards they cut up north."

"Cree?"

"Could be," said Iron Horn. "On the other hand, some of those half-bloods who sided with Riel ride unshod horses."

"Perhaps," said Robeson. "But to every white man west of the Missouri, it was Indians did this. Somehow it makes these people feel better . . . or worse, if it's your scalplock dangling from the belt of an Indian."

"Pershing—I shall leave a marker for him." Iron Horn swung down and found a few pieces of dried wood near a woodpile standing between the line shack and pole corral. He placed them on the ground in the shape of an arrow pointing northward.

Without warning, rifles opened up, one of the soldiers screamed in pain and fell over his saddlehorn, and Iron Horn felt a lead slug tear at his coatsleeve. He quartered his eyes around, but the way the wind was picking up and the snow was increasing, the Arikara couldn't tell where the shots were coming from.

"Dismount!" yelled Sergeant Robeson. "Open that corral gate and get our horses in there. Then get into the cabin."

Iron Horn ran his horse over to the corral and shouted, "They must think we're Indians."

"Well, damnit, you *are* Indians."

"Cree, those who were here before." Iron Horn ducked as a rifle slug punched into a corral pole near his head. "Can't see out there no more than a hundred yards, if that." He left his horse with others milling about in the corral, and broke with Sergeant Robeson and others toward the open cabin door. On the way there, one of the Arikara scouts clutched at his leg and dropped to his knees. A soldier and another scout grabbed him under the armpits and carried him into the sanctuary of the line shack.

"I figure it's some cowhands," said Robeson. "Damnit, they must know we're soldiers."

"Like I said on the way over here, they're liable to shoot at anybody and anything." Iron Horn crouched along with everyone else as slugs began pounding at the log walls of the cabin from all sides, some coming through chinks and a few seeking flesh through the two windows.

"Sounds like a whole army out there."

"I counted at least twenty guns," said Charley Ten Sleep. "Winchesters, some Henrys, a Sharps."

Grinning, Robeson said, "You've got a good ear for gun music."

"What's kept Charley alive all these years," Iron Horn said laconically. "And I've got a good idea as to who's out there."

"Chad Morgan must have brought his whole crew. They must have spotted us earlier today. Should have used more caution." Sergeant Robeson crab-walked to the potbellied stove and removed the lid. "No reason we can't have some heat in this place. Dillard, see if there's any food in that cupboard. Generally stock a place like this."

One of the buffalo soldiers brought his rifle up and sighted out through a crack in the window, but Iron Horn was there to yank the barrel down, and he said darkly, "The last thing we want to do is wing one of them."

"What if they try to rush us?"

"Return their fire, but aim high so you'll miss. I

figure Pershing should be here before nightfall. Sooner, once he hears gunfire."

Within a few minutes the firing tapered off, though every so often a bullet would plunk against the line shack to remind those inside to stay there. Since the line shack lay out in the open and on a lower reach of ground to protect it from the prevailing winds, after some debate Robeson and Iron Horn knew anyone attempting to get away and get word to Lieutenant Pershing wouldn't stand much of a chance, if any.

The day wore on, and with the heat coming up from the potbellied stove and the window shutters closed, a few unpleasant odors began circulating about. The lack of food and coffee didn't help dispositions, either. Trooper Caldwell blurted out, "My belly button's tickling my backbone. Sarge, I'm heading out to get my saddlebags."

Robeson snaked a glance out through a crack in a window. Visibility had lowered considerably in the time they'd been here, and he said, "Go ahead, but keep down."

Iron Horn muttered, "You'll need a little company." He set his rifle against the wall and strode behind Caldwell to the door. "Give us covering fire."

"I appreciate you doing this," said Caldwell.

Shrugging, the Arikara replied, "Just want to get at that whiskey bottle I've been toting along."

"And here," the trooper said sourly, "I thought you were going along to protect my hindside." Then he grinned and stole out the door with Iron Horn a step behind.

They got to the corral and inside before a wind-muffled shout was heard, and the ambushers opened up. Caldwell grabbed his saddlebags and a couple of others from horses beginning to whicker and wheel about in the circling confines of the corral. The grin left the trooper's face when a bullet lifted his hat away. Scrambling behind Iron Horn through the poles, they broke for the open door of the line shack, with rifle slugs punching the ground and air around them. Then Sergeant Robeson slammed the door shut and grimaced as a tattoo of bullets punched into its thick wooden panes.

Another hour passed, as did most of the sunlight trying to penetrate the billowing wintry clouds. It was then they heard a couple of horses whickering in agony, and poles being shattered as their cavalry mounts broke out of the corral and galloped away.

Iron Horn said simply, "We're afoot."

"Anyone who'd kill a good horse—" Robeson said angrily.

"Getting on to sundown," went on Iron Horn. "Once it gets dark we can break out of here."

Charley Ten Sleep cocked a questing ear and said, "I heard a bugle call . . ."

"Yup," exclaimed a trooper, "no mistaking that bugler of ours."

"Unshutter the windows," said Robeson as he stepped toward one, and he peered out into the dying shards of day, as did the others.

Rancher Chad Morgan and several of his waddies emerged from cover to wait for Lieutenant John Pershing and his buffalo soldiers. Morgan called out above the shrilling wind, "Better hold up there, Lieutenant. We've got some Indians trapped in that line cabin."

"For your information, Mr. Morgan," Pershing said upon reining up, "those are some Arikara scouts, along with my cavalrymen."

"To us," blustered the rancher, "they were damned renegade Indians . . . I figure some Cree."

"Let's just hope, Morgan, all of my men are still alive . . . and that includes the Arikara. Sergeant Murdock, hold the men here."

"You fixing to ride in alone?"

"Just like going to church, Morgan." John Pershing spurred his horse down the slope, and at his appearance, everyone began pouring out of the line shack. They gathered around as the man who commanded them brought his gelding up to the corral to stare at two dead cavalry mounts. The grim visage of Lieutenant Pershing swung to Iron Horn and Sergeant Robeson standing side by side.

"They let us come in before opening up," explained Iron Horn.

Sergeant Robeson reported that two of his men had been wounded.

"At least nobody got killed. Visibility isn't all that good out here." Pershing dismounted. "But I've the feeling that rancher didn't care if he killed an Arikara or a buffalo soldier. Sergeant Robeson, take my horse and go bring the others in. Then detail someone to round up your horses. We'll camp here tonight."

As Robeson swung into the saddle and cantered the gelding to the south, Lieutenant Pershing checked out the men who'd been wounded. Much to his relief, he found they weren't fatal wounds, but he also knew they must be taken in to Loma. He drew Iron

Horn aside.

"What have you got?"

"About all we found were tracks made by unshod horses."

"Coming in. Any trail leading out?"

"They went northward, Pershing. With the way it's snowing it'll be hard picking them up."

"But tomorrow, Kermit, we'll do just that."

FOURTEEN

They came, on a clear wintry day, to Rocky Boy's camp north of Bull Hook Bottoms, a large band of Cree led by Little Bear. Though Rocky Boy was glad to see his nephew, he pointed out to Little Bear that it would be almost impossible to give his Cree any food or shelter.

"We can hunt deer and elk, my uncle."

"The Chippewa have found few deer out on these frozen wastes. To find even one elk, or deer, we must go one day's journey."

They stood outside Rocky Boy's lodge buried like other tipis and crude shelters in deep snow. Naked trees gave these wanderers some shelter, and a short distance away lay a creek, but in order to get water each day, holes had to be chopped in the ice. The noonday sun was warming to their faces; it was a windless day, with the temperature somewhere in the high twenties. Both chiefs had blankets draped over their shoulders. Just to the west, Little Bear's warriors were setting up their tipis.

193

"My uncle," he began hesitantly, "I have talked to this man, Devlin."

"He has been here, too. Devlin speaks of the Chippewa, and Cree, being given land."

"He can be trusted."

"We must trust someone, or perish, my nephew."

Now, in a voice chipped with despair, he told Little Bear of how his people would steal at night to the slaughterhouses just outside Havre. "My people are eating the refuse from the slaughterhouses . . . and animals that had died from unnatural causes . . . carcasses that had not been destroyed. My people are forced also to live off the discarded rubbish of the white man. The winter is long, barely half over. I fear many will perish."

"Devlin has been speaking to the agent at the Blackfoot agency. Perhaps we will be allowed to go there."

"The Sioux and Atsina did not want us," countered Rocky Boy.

"All because Grass Bull couldn't control his temper. Now Grass Bull and others have gone . . . perhaps to join those with Coyote Walker."

"They are foolish," sighed Rocky Boy. "Now, Little Bear, what is this talk I hear of your Cree bringing down your women and children?"

"A son of Weasel Head found his way down to our camp, to tell us our people cannot survive up there— our women and children. They cannot go out hunting as in the old days. The soldiers keep watch over them. Even so, I have sent up some of my Cree to help them steal away."

"It is a long and dangerous journey."

Little Bear nodded and said, "Better my people perish down here than in a place of so much hatred."

"There is another thing, my nephew. The white man, Devlin, was here two suns ago. He told of how two men working at a ranch had been killed . . . Devlin said by Indians. I hope they weren't your Cree . . . or the Ojibwa, Coyote Walker. Because of this we cannot trade at Havre, nor be allowed to go begging on its streets, as some of my people have been doing. What a sad time."

At the moment, Coyote Walker watched impatiently the progress of two riders down along a snow-covered draw. He sat crosslegged before his campfire along the Marias River, warming his hands. There with him was Grass Bull, somewhat more stocky, with bold eyes the color of almonds, and with a cruel set to his wide mouth.

Their camp had been well chosen, an earthen wall protecting them to the northwest, escape routes opening onto the river southward, a game trail threading through willows and shrubbery and up the sloping wall of a draw to the east. It didn't bother these renegades that they lived in abandoned wood-cutters' cabins. Like the Chippewa somewhere to the east, they were having the same trouble finding game, and so they had stolen cattle and a few horses.

"These white men . . . you should not have told them how to get here."

In a dry, rattling voice, Grass Bull said, "They paid the Cree well for killing those white men out at that line shack. And they have come back, Coyote Walker, for the same reason."

"To kill again." A scowl wrinkled Coyote Walker's forehead as he thought out all of this. They had been on their way to join up with the Blackfoot westward around Browning and Dupuyier when Grass Bull and a few other Cree had appeared, after those white men had been killed. He'd found that the Cree ate like hungry pigs, that in a way they were an uncivilized bunch. But he let them stay here because there was strength in numbers. Another reason was that the Cree and Ojibwa had intermarried over the years, and thus blood bound them together. Still, Grass Bull's reputation was that of a man loyal only to himself, one not to be trusted for too long. On the other hand, these were not their ancestral lands in Canada, nor was it a time to make new enemies.

Grass Bull swung disdainful eyes to Ray Sharky and Yoke Rutel breaking their horses through some drifts pushing up against the corral. Drifting out of the cabins were warriors, some unarmed, the more cautious holding rifles and just itching to do something with them. They'd fattened up on stolen beef, whiskey brought before by these white men, and their own conceit. On the porch of a cabin one of the warriors let out a contemptuous fart, which provoked watchful smiles.

"Damned unfriendly lot," muttered Ray Sharky as he tied up his bronc and then swung his arms around to rid himself of a chill caused by the long ride from Havre.

"I don't like coming here, neither," complained his companion. Leaving his horse, Yoke Rutel urged the packhorse into a tired walk as he followed after

Sharky, trudging toward Grass Bull's campfire.

"Howdy, Grass Bull," Ray Sharky said with a forced joviality. "As I said, we're back with some supplies for you and your men."

Grass Bull motioned for the newcomers to sit down as he eyed the packs tied to the horses. "You have brought whiskey, bullets, food?"

"Exactly as you wanted."

Coyote Walker, although he could speak some of the white men's tongue, spoke rapidly to Grass Bull in Chippewa. "These men have bad eyes, especially the big one. Better we should kill them and take their horses and weapons."

The Cree laughed. "My good friend, Coyote Walker, welcomes you to our camp. You brought supplies; but we know you come for another reason?"

"The same as before." The hardcase dipped a hand into a sheepskin pocket to show the Indians a doeskin pouch. "You'll get more this time, Grass Bull. But no more cowhands this time. I want you to hit this ranch along Bullhook Creek. Place belongs to a man named John McCall; owns the Warbonnet Cattle Company."

"I do not know of this place."

"Me and Yoke'll guide you in. To get there it'll be safer to cut to the northeast so's to bypass Havre. That creek runs straight south of Havre for about twenty miles or so. McCall's main buildings are down there. I want you to be there five days from now."

"Five suns? As you wish, Sharky."

"How many warriors have you got to do the job?"

"We will have enough."

"Just be there." Ray Sharky rose and went behind Yoke Rutel to their horses. They had walked their broncs in, but when they left they cantered them back up the long draw passing southward.

Once in a while Yoke Rutel would twist in the saddle for a rearward look.

Grass Bull shaped a grim smile at this, and said, "They have given us some gold. And what is on this horse."

"They are stupid men," said Coyote Walker.

"Yes, as stupid as the Gros Ventre. But these supplies will help see us through the winter. And there will be more, for what reason I do not understand. But isn't it enough that we kill a few white men?"

"Are you asking me to join you, Grass Bull?"

"I am asking."

"My warriors thirst for revenge. Since we cannot take our anger out on those white settlers in Canada, let us slake our thirst for white man's blood down here."

FIFTEEN

The woman Desmond Kirby had installed in his rooms at the Western Hotel swung a languid hand over the side of the bed. Sunlight creeping through a window moved across the carpeted floor and spread over her face, and she came awake. She tossed the coverlet aside, a pouting gesture. Although possessed of a lissome figure and mane of tawny hair which at the moment was spread out on the pillow, the eyes in the thin face were jaded, the lips a little too compressed. Rose was the name given to her many years ago—she'd picked out Manchester from a book on English culture. Up until a month ago she had divided her working hours between a saloon on Chestnut Street, and streetwalking at night to pick up a few extra bucks.

"That bastard said he'd be back hours ago."

Then she smiled and stretched luxuriously. Though the man who'd made all of this possible was away a lot, when Desmond Kirby returned he usually trotted his mistress around town. And Rose Manchester liked nothing better than to slither from saloon to gambling casino on the arm of her paramour. He'd even given her enough money to buy a new wardrobe, and some to stow away for a rainy day. Which would be a long time in coming if Desmond Kirby lived up to his promise of taking her along when his business dealings here were completed.

During her time here, Rose Manchester had heard and seen some troubling things—those hired guns, for instance, and that angry encounter with a rancher, someone named McCall. Sometimes Kirby would tell her to take a stroll around town when certain gentlemen showed up. To her experienced eye they had all been cattlemen. She'd picked up enough to know Desmond Kirby was some kind of land agent. But the only thing that mattered to Rose was the color of his money. He seemed to have an inexhaustible supply of that.

Once in a while an officer had put in an appearance—a captain, as she recalled. Money had passed between them, but even so, it was apparent to her that the man who was keeping her distrusted this officer. This despite all of Desmond Kirby's charming smiles.

"Well, the bastard has charmed me into bed."

Another man, to whom Rose Manchester had taken an instant liking, was that Indian agent, Aaron Wilkerson. Here, though, Rose sensed, was a troubled young man. And on Wilkerson her paramour wasted none of his charm. When these two men got together it was as if an electrical storm was gathering over

Havre. Judging from what she'd garnered about him, Desmond Kirby was someone capable of many things, and that included murder. Wilkerson was idealistic, yet embittered. In her opinion, he possessed an inner strength as well.

"A couple of roosters just fixin' to get at each other. But sometimes that Kirby man can be ornery as a goat."

Since dealing with those Cree and traipsing back to Havre, gunhands Sharky and Rutel had been left to themselves by bossman Desmond Kirby. That had been yesterday, and ever since, they'd loafed at the saloons while the land speculator had been secreted with money men. For the pair of them this had been as though they were retired—doing some riding, but sticking burr-like to Kirby. As to why they'd been hired by Desmond Kirby, it all came down to some impeccable credentials. Each of their resumes had boldly scrawled in it the words murder and robbery; stagecoach and bank. There were testimonials to these bona fides from lawmen all the way north to Great Falls and down into Texas.

Damn, it made Ray Sharky proud just to ponder this.

In a couple of days they'd make tracks for Bullhook Creek to rendezvous with Grass Bull and his warriors. The trick was to keep from being spotted, as there were a couple of other ranches watering cattle in Bullhook, and generally a few cowhands were about. Farther south would be John McCall's place.

"Kirby has this all figured out."

"I don't get'cha," said Yoke Rutel.

"Them half-bloods."

Ray Sharky stared at his reflection in the mirror centered in the back bar. One boot was hooked on the railing, a cold stein of beer before him on the nicked bar top, and he had a smirk for Rutel. He had to admire the way Kirby had this figured. First it would be those Cree attacking the main buildings . . . slaughtering anyone they came upon . . . Then, before they cut and ran, LaVallier's half-bloods would take out Grass Bull and the other Indians. Then the buildings would be set on fire. Smoke from the burning buildings would fetch in John McCall's neighbors.

"Once they discover them dead Indians, the army'll take off after the rest of them Cree and Chippewa."

"Hope it works out as we planned."

"Just dummy up, Yoke. When you're drinking you're louder than a bass drum."

"No need," Yoke Rutel pouted, "to sass me out, Ray. I've been thinking."

"That a fact?" A doubting eyebrow shot up.

"Won't be too much longer before this is over . . . us working for Mr. Kirby. Don't know about you, Ray, but I've been livin' high off the hog, what with gambling and all. Been watching that bank on the corner. Couldn't help noticin' that's where the big businessmen and ranchers deposit their ill-gotten gains."

"Come to think on it, you're right. But just the two

of us?"

"Bumped into Willy Daggett the other day."

"So Willy's in town?"

"Him and a couple others. And tightening their belts, as they've fallen on hard times."

"Yoke, an extra nest egg will sure help." He clapped Rutel on the shoulder. "For once you came through. What say we go look up Willy Daggett and lay this out more."

Captain Morley Griffin hadn't expected to be sent out in the field, though he welcomed the chance to get away from Fort Assinniboine, even if it meant going with combined elements of the Tenth and Fifth cavalries. What he didn't particularly like was having to take orders from both Lieutenant John Pershing and Willoughby, a major from the Fifth Cavalry. Griffin knew that he was more or less on probation after the disgraceful way he'd acted at General Otis's home. Accompanying them from Fort Assinniboine, and at his insistence, was his daughter, Sallie. He had convinced her they should spend Christmas with old friends.

Wheeling out of line, he made his way back to his daughter, seated in one of the supply wagons. He tipped his hat and said, "This time John McCall brought his family into town. You've always gotten along with John's daughter, Cynthia. Besides, you need to be around someone your age."

"I was perfectly happy at Assinniboine," she snapped.

"Now, daughter, try to see it my way."

"You're doing this because of Aaron."

"Perhaps I am. Sallie, I know a good deal more about Wilkerson than you do. A lot more."

"Just what does that mean?"

His eyes grew cold, and he said, "I've told you enough for now. Just trust me."

The reason for their presence at a road junction that would bring them close to Havre were the orders from division headquarters that the leaders of both the Cree and Chippewa tribes were to be rounded up and then escorted to the border, where a contingent of Canadian troops was waiting. They'd learned of Rocky Boy's band settling in for the winter just to the northwest at Bull Hook Bottoms. Also, Chief Little Bear had brought most of his Cree there. Stretched out in columns of four were about two hundred cavalrymen. As custom dictated, they would make camp around midafternoon, for as always, the animals came first. Picket lines were set up for the horses and mules, and once again they were fed and watered. Thereafter, the men scattered to a variety of chores. Now they spotted chimney smoke lining out to the southeast, and a command echoed down the long line of horsemen and wagons indicating that a campsite had been selected in a low, shallow draw about a mile west of Havre.

Captain Griffin had been given permission to escort his daughter and her baggage into Havre, and as the column broke westerly, the brawny private sawing at the reins brought his wagon the opposite way on the main road.

Major Willoughby, a lanky Kentuckian, spurring his horse back, called out, "Hold up, Griffin." He cantered up with an anxious smile. "Would you be so kind as to buy me some smoking tobacco?"

"My pleasure." A silver dollar dropped into Captain Griffin's gloved hand. "Be back shortly." Then he reined around and cantered after the wagon.

With the departure of the major, Morley Griffin narrowed his eyes thoughtfully, letting his horse have its head as he went over what he planned to say to Desmond Kirby. First of all, that a lot of money must be backing Kirby's play, which could only mean someone influential in Washington City. But as long as big money was behind this attempt to take over the military reservation once the army pulled out, the efforts of Captain Morley Griffin must be appreciated a lot more. After all, hadn't he relayed to Desmond Kirby army directives that were meant for General Otis's eyes only? If that were found out, there'd be a court-martial and incarceration at Leavenworth. A bunch of cowhands veering around the wagon as they headed out of Havre brought a return wave from Captain Griffin and told him they'd just passed some outlying buildings.

"I suppose they'll be staying at the Commodore Hotel," Sallie Griffin said somewhat despondently to the captain edging up alongside the wagon.

This proved to be the case when, after turning off Cutler Street, they found the hotel and the McCalls waiting in their pair of upstairs rooms.

John McCall thrust out his hand, saying, "Captain, we had so much fun spending Christmas with you folks last year, well, we just had to return the compliment."

"Unfortunately, duty calls, John. At least for me." He had a wink for the rancher's daughter as he stepped over to grasp Jean McCall's hand and kiss her on the cheek. "This ranching life sure agrees with your wife, Mr. McCall."

"Out at Warbonnet my wife pretty much rules the roost. Now, Morley, what's this about duty calling?" He held out a glass of brandy.

"At last we have the authority to arrest some Indians."

John McCall's smile faded away. "Just what does that mean?"

He moved with the rancher into another room, and as he closed the door, Griffin said, "I left Assinniboine in command of the Fifth and Tenth cavalries. Right now my men are camped west of here. But tomorrow, John, we have orders to arrest all of the Cree and Chippewa leaders. We're to escort them back into Canada. Once that happens the rest of these . . . damned savages, are certain to clear out, too."

"About time."

"It's another ten days until Christmas. I figure a couple of days up to the border, the same back here. Which will give me plenty of time to be there for the festivities. Just to make sure, John, I'm leaving my Sallie as hostage. So, much obliged for the drink. And I do hope you'll take good care of my daughter until I get out to Warbonnet."

* * *

Captain Griffin threaded the boardwalks of Havre, tagged by lengthening shadows of a day wracked by a cold wind and subdued by an overcast sky. The one small glass of brandy shared with John McCall had whetted a sharp thirst, and but for the fact that the Western Hotel was just upstreet, he would have gone to any one of the saloons strung along the streets for a few drinks and a try at blackjack.

Ever since winter had set in, Morley Griffin had been restless, and even the smallest incident would lead to bitterness and an exacerbation of his somewhat explosive temper. He wasn't relishing the next few days spent in the presence of Lieutenant Pershing. Everyone from Commander of Western Forces Sheridan down to the lowest officer at Assinniboine shared the opinion that Pershing's star was on the rise. As Brevet Colonel George Armstrong Custer's had been. Perhaps Pershing's command would suffer a similar fate at the hands of these renegade Indians.

A bitter smile appeared, only to fade away when he veered around three men clustered on the boardwalk and caught the eye of U.S. marshal Sam Chapman coming out of a corner saloon. His pace faltering, Griffin nodded brusquely as the marshal said conversationally, "I hope someone's minding the store, Captain Griffin."

What was Chapman doing here? Generally this time of year U.S. marshals went into hibernation. Calm down, he told himself, for it could have something to do with those cowhands being killed by Indians. He felt no remorse over their deaths, just this hostility of the moment for Sam Chapman, and he said surlily, "Enjoying another game of poker, Marshal?"

Allowing an amused smile to appear, Chapman said, "I hope you're still not carrying a grudge over that little game we had at Assinniboine. I've found that into every life a little rain must fall . . . or a glass of whiskey can get a man just as wet." With a flourish, Marshal Sam Chapman eased the watch he'd won from the captain out of a vest pocket. "Lordy, how time flies. Almost past suppertime. You have a good day now, Griffin."

The marshal strode on, whistling softly, leaving an angry Morley Griffin staring after him. Through gritted teeth Griffin muttered, "Damn Chapman for his arrogance."

Overriding Morley Griffin's anger was a sense of cautious unease. The marshal could be up here looking for rustlers or other outlaws hanging around town. Griffin knew that he hadn't told anyone of his dealings with Desmond Kirby. What troubled him now were those two gunhands Kirby had hired. Unreliable men liking to get liquored up at the saloons. That big one, Rutel, as he recalled, often spoke out of turn. Kirby had brushed aside his query as to whether Sharky and Rutel had readers out on them.

Worriedly, he brushed past a carpetbagger just coming out of the Western Hotel, to catch the door before it closed. His glance took in one of the gunhands, Yoke Rutel, picking at his teeth from where he sat in an overstuffed chair. And from Rutel he learned that Desmond Kirby was up in his rooms.

Griffin's impatient rapping on an upstairs door found it being opened by Kirby's woman of the moment. She smiled brightly and said, "Why, Captain Griffin, how good of you to come." She was dressed for the evening in a red dress brushing against the carpeting and low enough to reveal her ample bosom, which jiggled as she stepped aside to allow him entrance.

From another room stepped Desmond Kirby, a drink in one hand, his jacket off, and one hand tucked into a pocket of his embroidered vest. He seemed pleased to see the captain, but above the easy smile were wondering eyes. "Rose, take the captain's coat and hat. Then be a good girl and go for a walk around town."

"Now, Desmond, honey, we're going out tonight."

"Don't we always." He turned and added, "Let's talk in here, Captain Griffin." He poured the captain a drink and talked in generalities until his mistress had left.

Morley Griffin went to the attack first. "I never expected this to take so long. Another thing: they couldn't find those Indians responsible for killing the two cowhands. Lost their trail in the snow, or so Lieutenant Pershing reported when he got back to Assinniboine. So, as far as anyone is concerned, Blackfoot or Sioux could have done the killing instead of those Cree."

"This is a risky business."

"And I've taken a lot of the chances. I could be court-martialed over this, drummed out of the army."

"Isn't that what you want, Captain—to get the hell away from that kind of life?"

"For my daughter's sake, yes."

"Griffin," he said sarcastically, "who are you kidding? The reason you threw in with me on this was because you're a compulsive gambler. Which, if the truth be known, is of little concern to me." He reached for a whiskey bottle. "And the reason our little venture is taking so long is because of foot-dragging in Washington City. My man there says we must proceed cautiously. I feel otherwise. This is a cold day to be traveling."

"I'm here with a contingent of soldiers who are encamped just outside of town. Seems orders came through at last to arrest the Indian chiefs and get them the hell out of Montana."

"Leaving the rest of the Cree and Chippewa behind," pondered Desmond Kirby. "Right here in Havre we have a lot of Indian sympathizers. So what we need right about now is an incident, something that will bring the wrath of the newspapers and everyone else in this territory down on these renegades."

"I suppose so," Griffin said sourly. "Another reason I came here is about my cut in this."

"You need more money," Kirby said plainly. "I expected this, Morley, and fortunately I can oblige you at the moment." From a table he picked up an envelope, then allowed Morley Griffin to eye its contents. "Five thousand, Captain."

Though his voice never betrayed his true feelings, in Desmond Kirby there was a contempt for Captain

Griffin and his kind. He felt the same way about Aaron Wilkerson, considered them tools to be used and then discarded. Just dangle a carrot before a man such as the captain and he'd sell his soul to have that and more. Of a more dangerous nature was rancher John McCall. In no uncertain terms McCall had called him a cheap hustler and con man, and had threatened further to find out why a so-called respectable businessman would have obvious hardcases hanging around.

So he'd decided John McCall had to die.

As for this unexpected visit from Captain Griffin, it brought to mind the details of a conversation they'd had at Fort Assinniboine. In a reminiscing way Griffin had told of the McCalls spending last Christmas at the fort, that Griffin and his daughter would honor the invitation to return the favor this year at McCall's Warbonnet Cattle Company spread. Desmond Kirby said casually, "Coming onto Christmas. Just another season of the year to me. You still planning, Captain, on going out to McCall's place?"

"As a matter of fact, Kirby," he replied, as he held out his glass to be refilled, "I left Sallie with the McCalls. Plan to head out there after we take care of this Indian problem. Oh"—he drank thirstily—"maybe you could tell me why Marshal Chapman is in town?"

"Chapman's here?"

"Bumped into the arrogant sonofabitch on my way up here."

Momentarily, this drew Desmond Kirby's train of

thought away from what he'd been about to tell Griffin. Crafting a smile, he said, "Outlaws are always drifting through. By the way, are the McCalls still in town?"

"They left so as to get home before it gets too dark. Why?"

The answer, which lurked in the mind of Desmond Kirby, was that his uninvited guest must be killed. He considered Captain Griffin's usefulness to be over. Partly because of Morley Griffin's greedy nature, the danger of being blackmailed at some future time.

"Quoting your words, Captain, you said this is taking a long time. This will change soon."

Captain Morley Griffin smiled back.

"Certain arrangements have been made." Kirby turned casually and went to stand by a wall cabinet abutting window curtains. He let his eyes play out the window to night settling upon Havre. Reflecting back at him in the windowpane were eyes that had become chiseled and unreadable. Without looking at his guest, he added, "The Cree are going to take out a ranch. Kill everyone there. Then others we have hired will ambush the Cree. Nice and tidy, Captain Griffin. Don't you agree?" He brought up a hand and placed it idly on one of the shelves within touching distance of a needle-pointed stiletto.

"Yes, I suppose so," Griffin said uncertainly.

"These Indians will hit this ranch around Christmas. A spread located south of here . . . some twenty miles or so." He turned just enough to smile at Griffin. "Isn't this what you wanted, Captain?"

212

"South of here?" The puzzled eyes of Morley Griffin suddenly widened. "My God, Kirby, you're talking of the Warbonnet . . ."

"So I am."

"My daughter will be there! No! I won't let this happen!" He dropped his right hand to pull up the flap on his holster, and was wrapping it around the butt of the single-action Colt when Desmond Kirby's arm blurred forward. The stiletto punched into the point of his stomach just below the ribcage and almost to the hilt. Reflexively the revolver lifted out of the holster, but it was too late for Morley Griffin. The shock of what had just taken place was etched all over the ashy face and in the disbelieving eyes. A final thought came: he was an officer, a . . . He pitched forward, but in death never felt the oaken floorboards coming up to smash into his face.

After a while, Kirby sauntered over and smiled down at the man he'd just killed, saying chidingly, "You'd become a loose end, my greedy captain."

He placed his glass on the table and, kneeling, turned the body over. Pulling out the knife, he wiped its blade on the captain's tunic. Then he picked up the army-issue revolver to place both the gun and knife in a desk drawer. Donning his coat, he went out into the hallway and made certain the door was locked before taking the staircase down to the lobby. As he'd expected, the gunhands were waiting in the barroom.

"Sharky, I've got a little chore for you and Yoke. Here's a key to my rooms. You'll find the captain waiting for you."

"Why didn't he come down here with you, Mr. Kirby?"

"It's difficult for dead men to take an evening walk."

"So you killed Griffin?" he said with a tinge of admiration.

"Here's what I want you to do with the body," The gunhands listened raptly to the words of Desmond Kirby.

"Never heard of that being done before. But I damned well know the Cree'll take to this like a whore to a double-eagle piece. Yup, downright diabolical, Mr. Kirby. And the body should keep in this cold weather."

"I trust there'll be no problems, Sharky."

"Nope, we'll get the body out of your rooms right away and head out for Bullhook Creek come sunup."

"Meanwhile, I have a dinner date with the luscious Rose Manchester." He smiled, and left them with a deeper respect for his killing abilities. Out on the street, Desmond Kirby suddenly remembered that U.S. marshal Sam Chapman was here, perhaps, as the late Morley Griffin had said, just on the hunt for some rustlers. Then he promptly shoved any thought of the marshal away as he began looking for his woman of the moment and a night on the town.

He reminded himself that on the day before Christmas a telegram must be sent down to Fort Assinniboine. It would detail how the Cree were planning to attack John McCall's home buildings. By the time the army reacted and sent cavalrymen over there, all they would find would be razed buildings and a lot of dead bodies, both white and Indian.

And, of course, they would puzzle over the presence of Captain Morley Griffin.

Desmond Kirby laughed at his macabre joke as he strode into a gaming casino.

SIXTEEN

A telegram had summoned U.S. marshal Sam Chapman to Havre—a telegram sent by police chief Mike O'Gallagher. Here, at Miles City, and in a few other bigger towns in the territory, it wasn't uncommon to see a uniformed policeman on the streets. Chapman realized, somewhat sadly, that in a few years, packing a gun would be a thing of the past. But, for now, men like him were needed to take care of the outlaw element. Somehow, too, just seeing a policeman on his beat made him think of bigger places, such as Chicago and St. Louis; maybe the West was becoming too tame a place for men like Sam Chapman.

The wire from O'Gallagher told of Willy Daggett's presence here, and that of two others wanted for a bank job in Rock Springs, territorial Wyoming. Right away Judge Wayland X. Zavier had ordered Chapman here, winter or no. While you're there, Judge Zavier had added, check in at Fort Assinniboine, just in case the army has picked up Grass Bull or other Indians wanted for killing and sundry crimes.

Running into Captain Griffin had been an unpleasant surprise. But earlier, he'd called upon Chief O'Gallagher at city hall and been told of how the captain had been keeping company with a land agent named Kirby.

"So why would Kirby be needing a couple of gunslicks?" O'Gallagher had asked at the time.

O'Gallagher had gone on to explain that Kirby's hired guns had been spotted at an eastside bar called Digger's, hovering around a table with the men Marshal Chapman had come to arrest.

Unexpectedly, Willy Daggett and those with him had disappeared. This was the reason Sam Chapman had been checking out the saloons. So far this evening, all he'd done was wear down boot leather. And he'd come alone, expecting any help he might need from Chief O'Gallagher.

"Here it's drifting on to Christmas," he mused, "and me darling Mag will have to spend it by her lonesome."

Marshal Chapman drew up at an intersection kitty-corner from the imposing Western Hotel, a cigar clamped between his teeth, with a silent question dusting his eyes. It was somewhere between ten o'clock and midnight. He knew that Captain Morley Griffin had gone into the hotel, just around sundown. The man could have left, for all he knew— gone back to join the Fifth and Tenth cavalries encamped someplace west of here, according to Chief O'Gallagher. And from Lieutenant John Pershing's description of land agent Kirby, that could only be

Kirby playing poker at a local casino with a painted Jezebel hanging on his every card. But of the captain there had been no sign.

Those gunhands of Desmond Kirby's—they could have come back to the hotel. He knew one of O'Gallagher's men was keeping an eye out for Sharky and Rutel; still, it wouldn't do any harm to meander across the street and have a look inside. Perhaps, with a little persuasion on his part, they would tell him where to find Willy Daggett. At least going into the hotel would beat standing out here fighting the cold. He crossed over.

Chapman was just opening the lobby door when a gun sounded, twice, followed by glass shattering. He bolted inside, brushing his coat open and unlimbering his sixgun. He ran through a hallway, then drew up short when a lead slug gouged the wall just ahead of him.

Pow-pow-pow!

He flopped down, and only when the gun fell silent did he realize the back door was being held open by a man straining to bring up his handgun. The thud of horses galloping away brought Sam Chapman to his feet and back to the door.

"Help . . . me."

"Easy," Sam said as he kneeled down. "You won't need that gun." He took it from the man's nerveless grip. "What happened?"

"Am . . . policeman."

"And I'm a U.S. marshal. Go on, son?"

"Saw . . . Ray Sharky . . . and . . . Rutel." The policeman's eyes closed as pain distorted his face. "Sharky . . . they . . . they . . ."

"Damn," Sam Chapman murmured as the policeman gasped and went limp. He felt for a pulse. "He's gone." Stepping around the body, he went out behind the hotel, and in the trampled snow came upon sign left by three horses. "Doesn't make any sense. There's only supposed to be two of them."

"Mister," shouted the night clerk as he appeared in the back door brandishing a shotgun, "you'd better have a good reason for being out here!"

"I'm Chapman," he said wearily, "a U.S. marshal. Son, you'd better call the undertaker."

Suddenly the night felt colder, and Sam Chapman a lot older. What was it Chief O'Gallagher had said—that he'd wired out descriptions of Ray Sharky and Yoke Rutel to other law enforcement agencies. A return telegram would probably be wired in tomorrow telling that these men were wanted in a lot of places. For certain, he would be out well before sunup to have a long talk with Captain Morley Griffin, as to his reasons for associating with that land agent.

But at the moment he had to tend to the body of a fellow lawman.

As Marshal Chapman had promised himself, he was saddlebound on the nightward side of false dawn. The big rangy sorrel hadn't liked leaving the warmth of the livery stable, and it kept getting gimpy-backed and acting skittish until Chapman brought it into a canter. The cold seemed to be all around him—in the way smoke hung low over the buildings, in the air with a frosty tinge to it, and what snow there was in Havre showing on a few rooftops and in whitish patches in front yards or vacant lots. The collar of his sheepskin was up and warming against his neck, and to make up for not having had his usual cup or two of chicory coffee, Sam Chapman was breathing in hot cigar smoke.

He had left talking to that land agent, Desmond Kirby, to Chief O'Gallagher, but he knew that Kirby would deny having been with his hired guns when that policeman had been gunned down. In a way, Sam Chapman had vouched for Kirby's whereabouts, as he'd seen him only moments earlier at that gaming casino. And the way that Jezebel had been hanging on to Kirby, she too was a bona fide alibi.

When he came to a fork in the road, with one route peeling southerly toward Fort Assinniboine, the other meandering off to the northwest, Sam pulled up and gazed straight ahead to where trees hovered along a draw. Even against the patches of snow he could make out the symmetry of army tents, the wagons, the slight movements of soldiers standing guard.

It was brighter now, but, even so, he went in at a walk, and had gotten to within a hundred yards when the metallic sound of a rifle bolt being thrown brought him up short.

"Who goes there?"

"Marshal Sam Chapman."

Then another sentry appeared, and both men walked out to look up at the marshal holding his badge in a cupped hand. "I'm Chapman out of Miles City."

"Yessir, Marshal, I saw you at Assinniboine. I'm afraid, sir, the officers haven't stirred yet."

221

"Hope there's a coffeepot warming someplace."

"Yup, as the cooks are up and about."

Even as they spoke, the encampment was stirring. There was a feel Sam Chapman had about an army bivouac—that nobody really slept, especially when in enemy country—this, and a sense of quiet order. He veered between the even rows of tents to find Lieutenant Pershing just stepping out of a larger tent, and behind him, a major. Swinging down, Sam walked his horse the rest of the way and ground-hitched the reins. Exhaling cigar smoke, he said, "A pleasure seeing you again, John." His grip was firm as they shook hands.

"This is Major Willoughby."

"Marshal Chapman," he drawled.

"You just come from Havre?"

"Spent the last couple of days there."

"By any chance did you happen to run into Captain Griffin?"

"Yes, about sundown last night."

"We expected the captain back within a couple of hours."

"Perhaps he preferred spending the night in a warm hotel room."

"Perhaps," the major replied. "And he might come riding in any minute."

They strolled over to a mess tent and helped themselves to coffee. Here, Pershing said, "You're not the only visitor we've had within the last couple of hours, Sam. A trapper blundered in. Claims he spotted a bunch of Cree up along the Marias River. Some Chippewa were there, too, and Blackfoot.

Their leader appears to be the Cree you're looking for—this Grass Bull."

"Wouldn't mind going up there and checking that out. Maybe you could lend me some of your soldiers."

"Unfortunately, we can't, Marshal Chapman," Major Willoughby cut in. "Our orders are to head farther north and take into custody some Indian chiefs."

"An opportunity of this sort might not come again until spring," argued Chapman.

Lieutenant Pershing said, "I see no harm in letting you have a couple of my Arikara. But according to that trapper, there were about thirty to forty Indians up there. I suggest you take them, Sam, and head for Assinniboine. There you'll have no problem getting all the troops you need to get at those Indians."

"Obliged, John."

"Iron Horn knows that country better'n most . . . and also you can take Charley Ten Sleep along."

Within a half hour Marshal Chapman headed out with an Arikara at either side. The sun was just about ready to dance over the black horizon eastward, while in a mellow sky wavy bands of pink billowed on patches of cloud. It showed promise of being a warmer day, and with the opportunity of going after the Cree with two fingers on his right hand, Grass Bull, thoughts about looking for hardcases were shelved, at least for the moment.

"How's it been, Kermit?"

"With my wives . . . or scouting?"

"Speaking of being hitched," said Sam Chapman.

"Reminds me that I was hitched to a woman one time . . . to the unsoiled dove of Ekalaka."

"It sounds like she must have been some woman."

"Iron Horn, she was an unholy terror. Which is the reason I've been unhitched ever since. Now, why don't you and Charley, here, give me the lowdown on what to expect up along the Marias . . ."

SEVENTEEN

Without Sallie Griffin around, the fort seemed like a barren wilderness, and the heart and thoughts of Aaron Wilkerson were heavy. Countless times he'd walked past that dark, empty house on Officers' Row, but there'd been no cheering light pouring out of the many windows. She had just left, without any explanation. But did Sallie owe him any? Her father, he'd decided, must have told Sallie all about Aaron Wilkerson's sordid past.

"Cheers," Aaron said to the lonely bartender on duty at the officers' club, but he said it quietly, bitterly. Even in his darkest despair he didn't want inquiring eyes on him.

He sank deeper into his chair at a lonely corner table, grasping his glass, and quoted silently from the Shepherd's Content: Love is a fiend, a fire, a heaven, a hell,/Where pleasure, pain, and sad repentance dwell.

Here he was, wracked by self-pity at having fallen in love, and for having succumbed to the dictates of his uncle. Thinking back, Aaron realized that being in prison was far better than doing the bidding of Secretary Josh Tremont.

After Lieutenant Pershing had returned, the talk at Assinniboine had been of those killings. Two innocent men, cowhands, killed for nothing more than greed. Afterwards, too, there still lurked in his mind the thought of how Captain Griffin had carried on with his duties as if nothing had happened. The father of the woman he loved. But he'd been told about it, and out of fear for himself, had done nothing.

Had he sunk so low?

Aaron considered having another drink. He had found it helped him escape from a lot of things. But even all he'd consumed failed to wipe out how he felt about himself. Heaving himself out of the chair, he found a side door and early afternoon sunlight touching down upon Assinniboine. On a pathway he hesitated. Not wanting to go to the loneliness of his quarters, Aaron struck easterly toward his office, just a stone's throw from post headquarters.

There, he stoked the fire before settling down behind his desk. He shuffled some papers, shoved them away, brought his chair swiveling around and stared out a window giving him a view of a few officers and enlisted men passing in and out of the headquarters building. Shortly thereafter, a man he vaguely recalled as having been here before rode up and swung down, as did one of the Arikara scouts.

Wait a minute . . . yeah, that was a U.S. marshal— Chapman, he thought.

He watched the scout and Chapman enter the

building. Now it dawned on him that he could end all of this by simply going over and confessing his part in this land scheme to Marshal Chapman. Drinking had put him in a reckless, uncaring mood.

"Or better yet," he said, "pack up and head west. Sallie left without saying goodbye. What's left for me here?"

This sudden decision brought Aaron Wilkerson to his feet. From his desk he removed a few personal possessions, which he shoved into coat pockets. Donning his coat and hat, he left, but this time with a bitter smile.

Major Dan Crowley beckoned the marshal and the Arikara scout into his office. Motioning toward chairs, he said to Kermit Iron Horn, "I thought you left with Lieutenant Pershing."

"Iron Horn left with Pershing," the Arikara stated.

"Then," said Marshal Chapman, "we found out the Cree I've been looking for is holed up someplace along the Marias River." He went on to tell of the recent events. "So, Major Crowley, Grass Bull has gathered about twenty or so men around him. According to this trapper, these Indians have been stealing a lot of horses and cattle. We get Grass Bull and all of this will cease. Mind if I smoke?"

The major smiled his approval. "What you'll need is at least two companies." Rising, he stepped to a wall map. He found the river and gauged the distance up there, as Iron Horn stressed that it would be tough going once they came upon the breaks radiating out from the Marias. Crowley added, "At least two days to get up there; that is, if the weather holds."

"We have a pretty good idea of where they're holed up."

"Even so, you'll need provisions for a week or more. General Otis was called away to division headquarters. That leaves me in charge out here, gentlemen, which means that unfortunately I can't go along."

At that moment a lieutenant stuck his head into the room and said, "Sir, this telegram just arrived." Advancing into the room, he handed the yellow envelope to Major Crowley, who tossed it down on his desk.

"Lieutenant," said Crowley, "Alert Companies B and F they'll be leaving this afternoon for an expedition up along the Marias River. They'll need provisions for at least . . . two weeks. Just packhorses, Lieutenant."

"I couldn't ask for more," said Sam Chapman as the lieutenant left, and the major tore an end away from the yellow envelope.

Curiously Major Dan Crowley's eyes dropped to the unfolded sheet of yellow paper he held. It took a moment for what he'd just skimmed over to filter into his thoughts, and only then did his face harden as he said, "I don't know if this is some kind of joke or not, Marshal Chapman."

He passed the telegram to Chapman, who read out loud, "Party of Cree led by Grass Bull plan to attack J. McCall ranch tomorrow." He laid puzzled eyes on Crowley. "It doesn't say who sent this. But I don't think we can just ignore it."

The major spun to the map as the others rose and

came over. "The McCall ranch? Yes, south along Bullhook Creek. It's shown here as the Warbonnet Cattle Company." His eyes narrowed thoughtfully. "Yes, as I remember it, Chapman, Captain Griffin was going to spend Christmas out at the McCall ranch. His daughter, Sallie, is there now."

"Kind of strange the Cree would hit that place on Christmas day. Unless the person who sent this telegram is behind all of this." For some unaccountable reason, all Sam Chapman could think of at the moment was how Captain Griffin had been involved with that land agent at Havre. What kind of crooked deal were these men involved in? This telegram could only mean they had had a falling-out. Wait a minute—there was that shooting at the Western Hotel; those gunhands of Kirby's killing that policeman. Two hardcases, and tracks left by three horses. It all came together for Sam now; the third horse belonged to Captain Morley Griffin. But why the shootout, unless they were abducting the captain or were taking his body out of the Western Hotel?

And those two cowhands killed westward on Chad Morgan's ranch, at the hand of Grass Bull. Why? Just random killings? He shrugged that away, for there had to be a deeper reason. This telegram made even less sense to Marshal Chapman as he studied the map. It showed the boundary lines of Fort Assinniboine Military Reservation. Along with the different mountains situated on this land, Sam noticed, the many creeks and wide areas of grassland, as detailed on the map, would make it ideal grazing land.

"Major, I've heard in a roundabout way Assinniboine is going to be abandoned by the army."

"It is, Sam."

"That some folks around here want a big chunk of this land given to these Indians."

"Efforts are being made in that direction. Most of this talk comes from the Bureau of Indian Affairs back east. And there have been articles in the newspapers stating that some Congressmen are in favor of this."

"What you just said ties all of this together. And the reason for this telegram." He handed it back to the major. "Someone has hired Grass Bull and his Cree to go on a killing spree. I'll bet the Cree will still be there when we get over to the McCall ranch. Meaning we'll arrive just in time, I'm hoping, to take them out. Once word of this gets out—that the Cree slaughtered those people over there—it'll end all of this talk about Assinniboine becoming an Indian reservation. Pronto, the rest of the Cree and Chippewa will be clapped in irons and sent back to Canada . . . and to hell with what the Canadian government thinks."

"Damned if you're not right, Sam," Major Crowley said tersely. He went over and opened a closet door, lifted out his coat and hat. "It's going on three o'clock. And a good seventy miles to the McCall place."

"Major, I tell you what. Me and Iron Horn will go on ahead."

"But I'll need a scout."

Said Iron Horn, "Charley Ten Sleep is sitting his horse outside. Ten Sleep knows that country better'n me."

"Very well, Charley will go with us."

Marshal Chapman said, "With you going, who's gonna take charge here?"

"My orderly, damnit." He marched out of his office and down the long hallway, with Chapman and Iron Horn stepping fast in order to keep up.

The strident call of a sergeant caused Aaron Wilkerson to look over at the stable area as he tightened the saddle cinch. Stowed in his saddlebags were a few articles of clothing, a few personal effects, and a handgun that he used only for target practice, one of his few diversions here at Assinniboine.

First that U.S. marshal had arrived, and now at least two companies were saddling their horses. But this was no concern of his. His greatest fear was of running into Marshal Chapman before he could get through the main gates, because Aaron was torn between telling the marshal what he knew, or just cutting out. Doing so, he realized, would make him an accessory to the murder of those cowhands. And out here that was a hanging offense.

Just thinking about this brought Aaron into the saddle. A cold wind beat at his fur cap and slapped across his face, and he knew it would be a long and cold ride to wherever he was going. Southwesterly, he thought; down to Billings, where he'd exchange the horse for a train ticket. From there on, it was a random destination. The route he took brought Aaron alongside the stables, where he encountered a sergeant who had been kind enough to show him the rudiments of handling a weapon at the firing range.

"Sergeant Kincaid, you going someplace?"

"Oh—Aaron—yup, heading out to some ranch east of here. Let's see, yeah, John McCall's place. Got the word it's gonna be attacked by Indians."

"I see," he murmured, as for some strange reason he got to thinking about Sallie Griffin, and some chance remark she'd made earlier this month. With a wave for the sergeant, he set his horse into motion. McCall? Nope, didn't ring a bell. By chance—or it could have been from force of habit—he swung his eyes toward Officers' Row; there in the windows of a house were Christmas decorations, and there was a green, beribboned wreath hanging from the front door.

Christmas . . . rang a bell? Yes, that rancher and his family had spent last Christmas here . . . at Sallie's. This year the Griffins were going to— His blood ran cold, and he paled as the realization of what that meant struck home.

Now he spotted Marshal Chapman and an Arikara scout loping their horses toward the main gates and, without thinking, he spurred after them. A few curious eyes watched Aaron Wilkerson gallop his horse across the parade grounds, as he shouted, "Chapman! Marshal Chapman!"

Drawing back on the reins, Chapman wheeled his horse around, as did Kermit Iron Horn. As Aaron came up, the marshal said, "Now just what is troubling you, son?"

"Marshal, I'm . . . I'm a friend of Sallie's . . . Sallie Griffin. She's at the McCalls', along with her father. And I reckon that's where you're going."

"We be that."

"I want to go along."

"Any particular reason? As I recollect, you're Wilkerson."

"Yes, Aaron Wilkerson, the Indian agent here. Or I'm supposed to be one. Look, Marshal Chapman, it's a long story."

"Probably a heap longer to McCall's place. We'll be riding hard, Aaron, through what's left of today and all night. Someone not used to this pace could slow us up."

"I must get there. Don't worry, I'll keep up."

"Then let's ride."

EIGHTEEN

Rancher John McCall could feel the crisp morning air snapping at his nostrils when he came out on the back porch and took in the layout of his many buildings. Just five years ago there'd been only the one hip-roofed barn and a few other buildings. Presently he'd been able to add another barn, a couple more corrals, and a tack house to replace one that had burned down. This land had treated him well, since he'd paid it back by not trying to plow up some acreage as others were doing; instead, leaving it as nature intended, in long, rolling grassland. Near the barns were several haystacks, with more hay up in the lofts. Whatever sweet feed he needed was purchased at Havre. Almost two years ago, McCall had strung barbed wire to enclose the home buildings. Other fence lines ran across his large range.

He strode into the back yard, hatless, wearing a sheepskin hanging open despite the chill, which would go away somewhat when the sun stopped fooling around and rose. But this was the time of the day he liked best—calm before the wind came in, and if a man sharpened his hearing, he just might catch the last sounds of the night creatures. Just yesterday morning he'd heard an owl letting go by the trees growing along the creek, and suddenly, there it was, ghosting in past the barns and spearing John McCall with those big, unblinking, green eyes.

Since winter range had been moved closer to the buildings, the hands he'd kept on lived in the bunkhouse stretched out between two big oak trees. He gazed at smoke spiraling out of the chimney, lantern light pushing through the windows, and an envious gleam came into McCall's gray eyes. That's what he had been some time back, a footloose waddy. Despite the sudden yearning to have that kind of life again, the sense of pride at what he now had rose in him. More than anything, it was his wife, Jean, who had made all this possible. How she had put up with him for a couple of long years in that sod house was still a mystery, but she had, and now they had wrested out of this land a rambling house containing some fifteen rooms. And this spread, the Warbonnet.

As he was on the verge of going back into the ranch house, one of his waddies emerging from the bunkhouse held John McCall there; he recognized the hand as Brady Gant, his foreman. Sighting his boss, Gant ambled over and said, "Kind of a cold morning, John."

"Some, but it'll warm considerable. And it's Christmas day. Meaning you and the others will eat up at the main house."

"Obliged for that. Wasn't that captain supposed to be here?"

236

"Expect Captain Griffin most any time. He'll probably come riding in today. How's that gelding?"

"As you suspected, it's got chronic indigestion. I've changed its feed, and have been giving it cinchona. Coming along just fine now."

Nodding, the rancher swung around on the narrow walkway and went into the house, and his *segundo* headed back toward the bunkhouse. In his late thirties, Brady Gant was lanky, with the slow, easy mannerisms of a man accustomed to this kind of life. He didn't smoke, but chewed tobacco.

Now he paused before entering; the crow's-feet deepened around his probing eyes as they took in the creekward approaches to the home buildings. There, it came again, just a whisper of sound, but enough to arouse his curiosity. Could it be an owl? he mused after a while. Despite the cold, he held there, since it was entirely possible some of those Indians who'd been driven out of Canada had come down this way seeking to rustle some cattle. He couldn't think of any other reason for their being here. Any factor that held Brady Gant outside the bunkhouse was a reminder of how his parents, and his only brother, had been killed by Indians. This had been back when the Plains Indians still ruled the roost out here.

"And not that Godawful long ago," he said quietly. A searching glance quartered most of the buildings and other approaches to this place, but what struck Gant the most was how terribly quiet it had become, like a lull before a storm. That got him to thinking about those two cowhands of Chad Morgan's being taken out by Indians. He let his eyes drift around for a final look before shouldering into the bunkhouse.

In various stages of getting dressed were six other cowhands, and now what their *segundo* said took all of them by surprise. "Hustle into your duds, boys. Then strap on your sidearms and check out your rifles."

Snorting through his handlebar mustache, Clark Murdock said, "You getting addled in your old age, Gant?"

"Something's out there," he said quickly, striding over to his bunk, where he lifted his holstered gun out of his warbag. He began strapping it around his waist. "Maybe those same Indians who took out two of Morgan's hands. But we can't afford to take any chances."

"You are worried, Brady?"

"Mostly playing a hunch. But it's too damnable quiet out there . . . so much so, it made chills crawl up my back. They probably know we're in here. What they're waiting for is for us to go about our mornin' chores. Once we're spread out and away from our guns they'll hit us. The barns are a far piece from the ranch house . . . so nobody goes that far. Two of you saunter easy-like over to the tack house. Murdock, you and Steve head for the grainery, turn on one of the lanterns as though you boys were filling gunny sacks with feed. The rest stroll with me over to the main house. This way, when those red devils come in, we'll have them in a crossfire."

"But what if there's nothing out there?"

"Then all of us are going to enjoy a turkey dinner and all the trimmings. Before going out, boys, conceal your long guns under your coats. Okay, Murdock goes first, then Casey."

Quickly they got ready, and in leaving the bunkhouse, turned out the lantern. The last to leave was Brady Gant, who made casual conversation with the two waddies just a step behind on the narrow walkway. Their presence in the back kitchen lifted the eyebrows of Ma Campbell, the cook, and Jean McCall just coming back to refill a coffeepot.

"Brady?" Then, as he opened his long coat, she saw the rifle, and that those with him were also carrying rifles along with their leathered sixguns.

"Tell John I'd like a quiet word with him, Mrs. McCall."

Without saying anything, she handed the empty coffeepot to Ma Campbell and shoved through the swinging door. In a moment the rancher was there, and his *segundo* said, "Something may have spooked me, John, but I know there's something out there."

"Indians, I expect."

"No sense taking any chances."

"Or it could be Captain Griffin coming in?"

"Could be, but I heard too many owls hooting for my liking. I've got two men in the tack house, two in the grainery."

"Get them in a crossfire," agreed John McCall. He lifted a curtain aside and glanced outside. "Still kind of hazy. If they're there, boys, they'll come in when it clears more. Maybe in a half hour or less." He threw his men a smile. "Better start closing the shutters." He went ahead of his men into the spacious living room.

Sallie Griffin, sitting at the oaken table with the rancher's daughter, Cynthia, sensed that something was wrong, but being used to the army way of things, managed to keep her composure. She placed her napkin alongside her plate and reached out to pat Cynthia's hand.

"This is really a solid house," said Sallie.

"Yes, I know. But it's been so long since we've had this kind of trouble. That is, if any Indians are out there."

"You girls," said Mrs. McCall, "come over by the fireplace."

"I wonder what's keeping my father?"

"Don't worry, girl, the captain will be here. You'll see."

Out in the grainery, Clark Murdock doused the lantern, since it was getting light enough to see without it. But he'd sent the other waddy with him to keep watch out a window opposite the open grainery door. Easing up to the door frame, he stole a glance eastward and found that mist was rising from along the creek. He was more nervous than he'd been in a long time. Somehow he had to trust Gant's notion that at any minute they would be getting some unwelcome guests. It had been a long time since any of them had seen Indians on the prowl, despite the fact that some Warbonnet cattle had been stolen this fall.

At first Clark Murdock wasn't sure if he'd seen anything; then a horseman appeared so suddenly he almost let go of his rifle. Just the one rider, heading in away from the creek and sitting his saddle kind of awkwardly. "Rider's coming in!"

"Still don't see anything to the northeast, though."

"Keep your eyes peeled," warned Murdock.

Lashed to the saddle of the running horse was the body of Captain Morley Griffin. The Cree had stuck a broken limb down the back of his army coat to hold him erect in the saddle, and the dead captain's arms dangled back and forth to spur on the frightened horse. Murdock broke outside in an attempt to stop the runaway horse, but stopped short when John McCall yelled at him from the front porch of the house.

"Get back! Some Indians are coming in!"

Murdock wheeled, and then he saw a wave of horsemen sweeping in from the west. The Cree and Chippewa with them were spread out in a ragged, yelping line, and some of them cut loose at the cowhand scrambling back into the grainery.

Gasping his fear away, Murdock said, "Guess Gant was right after all. Don't fire yet. Let those bastards come in closer . . . that's it . . . okay, pour it into them."

The marauding Indians cut along the wide open space between the main house and the grainery and tack house. They weren't expecting what happened now—guns firing back at them. Several toppled out of saddles and some horses received hits.

At a shouted command from Grass Bull, they took off after him, swerving toward the barns. A few random slugs poured after them before the Indians were out of sight. Quickly the tack house and grainery were vacated, the waddies running toward the main house.

"What in tarnation do you make of that soldier?"

"That was an officer."

"But a dead one."

"Damnit," cursed Murdock. "It had to be the girl's father."

"That horse carried him over by the barns. Yeah, there it is now. What do you think, Clark?"

"Anybody foolish enough to go over there will be just as dead. I just hope the girl didn't see that."

But Sallie Griffin had caught a glimpse of the officer pounding past the house on the runaway horse, and her frightened scream pierced through the house. At the moment, she sat slumped by the fireplace, Mrs. McCall trying to comfort her, the men by the shuttered windows and bracing for another assault by the Indians. Sallie cried out, "I . . . I . . . What have they done to him?"

John McCall's boots thudded on the hardwood floor. Then he knelt down by her chair and said, "They must have run into the captain on their way down here. Sallie, he was a soldier; he didn't go down without a fight."

"It was . . . just horrible." She closed her tear-rimmed eyes. "He so wanted to be here for . . . Christmas."

The others were in the kitchen now, spreading out to take up positions by windows. Then Gant yelled that fire was pouring out of the barns. Giving Sallie a comforting pat on the arm, John McCall went over and peered out a window, the anguish of what he was feeling planted on his wind-scoured face. He ran a disgusted hand along his hairline and said, "This doesn't make any sense. You boys have seen Indians before."

"For sure they weren't Sioux or Blackfoot or even Gros Ventre."

"Atsina?"

"Nope, not hardly likely. Got to be those damned Cree, John."

"I've a hunch you're right, Gant. And we have you to thank for being alive. I owe you for that one. Why?" This was said more to himself than anyone else in the room.

"I don't need this field glass now," groused Marshal Sam Chapman as he stared eastward at thick smoke staining the morning sky. "We're still about a mile or two out."

Iron Horn said, "We haven't heard any shots for a while. Could be it's over."

"No," said Aaron. "I know they're still alive."

"Strange."

Chapman looked over at the Arikara. "What have you got, Kermit?"

A sweep of Iron Horn's hand to the southwest revealed another group of horsemen converging on the ranch buildings, and by the time Marshal Chapman had focused in on them with his field glass the new arrivals were spreading out and unsheathing long guns. "What in tarnation are those wastrels up to?" He adjusted the lens on his field glass. "I'll be a ring-tailed wonder, Kermit. They're half-bloods!"

"They didn't just happen to be out here."

"Are you thinking what I'm thinking?"

"That once the Cree get done with their killings, the half-bloods move in and take them out."

Chapman replaced the field glass in a saddlebag as he said, "How far back do you think the cavalry is?"

"Couple of hours, maybe more."

"Suppose so. Anyway, what's our hurry? Haven't heard any guns for some time now. And you know what that means."

Aaron Wilkerson said angrily, "We just can't wait out here for the others to show up." Then his anger dissolved when guns began sounding again. "I told you they were still alive."

"You must really love that Sallie girl."

"Until now, I didn't know how much. Well, Chapman, what's it gonna be?"

"Son, you are awful disrespectful toward an old gent like me. Since Kermit and I want to keep our scalplocks, at least until more gray hair sets in, we'll have to keep from being spotted by both those half-bloods and the Cree. Meaning, if you agree with this, Kermit, we work our way around to the north, then come in. That gully yonder will do nicely. But after that, it's mostly out in the open. You game for this, son?"

The response Aaron gave was to jab spurs into his horse and bring the tired animal into a canter. Smiling at each other, his companions set their horses into motion.

Down in the gully, Sam Chapman said, "That land agent is one clever rascal. Getting those half-bloods to do his dirty work by killing off their old comrades-in-arms. Not to speak of killing Captain Griffin."

Aaron blurted out, "The captain is dead?"

"Way I figure it, Aaron. Otherwise, he would have come back to camp. Should have told you before, but guess I had other things on my mind. And I figure it's my responsibility to break the news to his daughter."

"No," he said bitterly, "I'll do that. I'm as much responsible for Captain Griffin being killed as that land agent, Kirby."

They rode out of the gully as the marshal said, "You can tell me about this later, son. Less'n a half mile to them buildings, and not much shelter. But it'll help if we angle toward the creek. That way, if we're spotted, at least those trees'll give us cover."

Astride their tiring horses, the three of them decided it was time to unlimber their guns. As yet they hadn't been spotted, and Iron Horn mused that it was because the marauders were too busy trying to take out those defending the buildings. Flames still rose from the burning barns, and the haystacks had caught fire; the wind picked up and swirled smoke about to give them some cover.

It was Iron Horn who spotted one of the Cree keeping watch over war ponies lodged in a pole corral. In one smooth motion, the Arikara brought up his rifle. The lead slug dropped the Cree where he stood watch by the corral gate. Iron Horn said, "Might as well turn them ponies loose."

"Might's well," agreed Chapman.

Once this was done, with Marshal Chapman in front, they walked their horses behind a shed. Off to their right was the tack house, farther along the bunkhouse, while scattered about in places of concealment were those Indians led by Grass Bull. In the big ranch yard they could see a few bodies and two dead horses, and they heard the reverberation of guns.

"Aaron, those horses are too spent to go another

foot. Just the same, you can stay here or help us take out some of these killers."

Hefting his handgun, Aaron said, "Show me the way, Marshal."

Nodding, Marshal Chapman turned and followed after Iron Horn, easing along the shed wall. Farther along was a woodpile, behind which they crouched. Now they could pick out a couple of Cree here, some Chippewa yonder, so engrossed in their killing work that they hadn't bothered to throw a glance toward their backtrail. Softly, Chapman told them to pick out targets and commence firing.

Swiftly, and with deadly accuracy, Marshal Chapman and the Arikara fired at their targets while working the levers on their rifles. Aaron Wilkerson's first bullet plunked into a grainery wall. The next effort from his handgun thudded into a Cree's head to explode the top away, and the Indian slumped over.

It was the Chippewa, Coyote Walker, who sensed the new danger. Flopping around from where he'd been hidden behind a large oak tree, he fired toward the woodpile. Springing up, he fired the rifle from his hip, only to have a slug from the marshal's weapon slam him backward to the ground. One of the Indians yelled a warning, which seemed to echo the distant trumpeting of a bugle. Confused now, the Indians broke away, and Grass Bull appeared briefly but ducked behind the tack house when Iron Horn let go at him.

"You want him alive, Marshal?"

"Iron Horn, any way I can get him. But Grass Bull won't get far without a horse."

Other Indians broke into the open; some went down and others took to shelter again. Then a bugle blared as a long line of cavalrymen came toward the buildings. Within minutes, they had rounded up the marauding Indians. But they did not take Grass Bull alive, for his body was found close to the burning barns. When Marshal Chapman looked around, it was to find young Aaron Wilkerson heading for the ranch house and those who'd defended it coming out to welcome their rescuers.

Major Dan Crowley put in an appearance, and as he swung down, he said to Marshal Chapman, "We came upon the captain's horse out yonder. Griffin was still in the saddle. A terrible way to die, Marshal."

"These Indians didn't kill Captain Griffin."

"I don't understand."

"Griffin was killed up at Havre. Probably by the same man who's responsible for what just took place here. And Havre is where I'm heading, Major Crowley."

Coming around the grainery, Aaron Wilkerson pulled up when he saw Sallie standing near the front porch of the main house. With the woman he loved were two other women, while spreading out in the yard to take a closer look at the dead Cree and Chippewa were rancher McCall and his cowhands. Aaron hesitated, wanting to run over and sweep her into his arms. Then she spotted him, and yelled out as she ran toward him, "Aaron . . . oh, Aaron . . ."

He broke into a run, and Sallie Griffin suddenly came into his arms, sobbing so that her body shook. He said, "Thank God you're alive. When I saw the fire I thought the worst. Oh, Sallie, how I love you."

"My father . . ."

"The marshal told me. Darling, I'm so terribly sorry." He pulled out of her arms, threw her a searching look. "There's something I have to do."

"What do you mean, Aaron?"

"Please, I . . . I must go."

NINETEEN

After three years, Aaron Wilkerson knew the routine by heart: the guards making that final check of his cell block at precisely ten o'clock, at which time all lights were doused. So started another lonely night at Old Capital Prison.

But on this summer night in early May, Aaron was more than eager for the lights to be turned out, for in the morning he would be released from prison. He had made no plans beyond the day of his release, nor did it matter to Aaron where he would go. Many a time he had thought about Marshal Sam Chapman and that last ride with the marshal into Havre, Montana Territory.

Bolstered by Havre policemen, there'd been a brief firefight with Desmond Kirby's hired guns, one being wounded, the other killed. Later Ray Sharky had been hung, as had the land agent, Kirby. But at the time, Kirby didn't resist when Marshal Chapman came to his hotel room. He could still remember the smug look on Desmond Kirby's not unhandsome face, for what could happen to him, since he had the backing of Secretary Josh Tremont? What did occur was that Aaron turned state's evidence, with the trial held right there in Havre. Aaron's testimony had helped to put his Uncle Josh behind bars. Then, to Aaron Wilkerson's dismay, he was taken back to Washington City, there to serve out the rest of his original sentence.

Of Sallie Griffin he had seen little, both at that trial in Havre and afterwards. There was an opportunity to speak to her just after the trial ended, and he tried telling the woman he loved how so much of what had happened had been his fault. Sallie hadn't said a whole lot, but when he had had his say, she had turned and left him standing in the emptying courtroom. He had never felt lonelier.

It seemed to Aaron that he had scarcely closed his eyes when the familiar tread of boots on concrete vibrated in the cell block. Earlier than usual, he felt. Only this time the pair of guards had come for him, and eagerly he walked between them to where he would receive his old clothing and the traditional five-dollar bill. Afterwards, he was brought out to the main gates, which seemed to barely creep open; then he bounded through the opening, with the single valise containing his worldly possessions and the money given to him in a pocket.

Vehicular traffic along the street in front of the prison was light this early in the morning, but as he set out bravely in an attempt to cross the wide thoroughfare, a waiting carriage pulled away from the curbing and clattered up to him. He glanced that way, thinking it was a handsome cab, only to hear a voice from the past.

"Aaron, please wait."

Turning, he murmured in disbelief, "Sallie?"

The side door opened and Sallie Griffin emerged, somewhat older, but to him, as beautiful as ever. He stepped closer, drank in her face and eyes, the way she now wore her hair, while inwardly there was a part of him that he held in check. Wasn't this the woman who had rejected him at Havre? He stood there, not knowing what to do or say. Perhaps he should simply walk away.

"Please, Aaron, please forgive me for the way I acted. You must understand that I rejected your love because of what happened to my father. I was young then, Aaron, as you were. Can you ever forgive me?"

"It is you who should forgive me . . . for being such a coward. I . . . I . . . ."

Reaching up a gloved hand, she touched him on the cheek. What she felt about him shone out of eyes starting to swim with tears. Then she brought her lips to his, and for Aaron Wilkerson, suddenly everything was all right.

"Dearest, I should have written . . . a thousand times."

"None of that now."

"But I didn't think you'd want to hear from me again . . . see me again."

"You're here—that's all that matters."

"Aaron, I have some money; my father's inheritance. And you often spoke of Oregon—"

"Oregon it shall be, then." Suddenly aware of his shabby appearance, Aaron smiled wearily. "I seem to recall this happening to me before—my being

251

unexpectedly released from this very prison . . . and then taking a train to Chicago, wearing other shabby attire. But unlike that time, you are here now, Sallie."

"And to me you look like a man of means. My carriage awaits, my love."

"And Oregon."

EPILOGUE

Lieutenant John J. Pershing did escort the Indian chiefs from the Cree and Ojibwa tribes back to Canada, and they stood trial in Ottawa for their crimes, only to be released because of unreliable witnesses to what had actually happened during the Meti's rebellion. Later, all of the combined tribes of the Cree and Chippewa were escorted to the international border, and to the amazement of Lieutenant Pershing and other officers, when they returned they found the same Indians camped near Havre. Time after time the Indians were taken to the border, and as often they returned. They would, it seemed, much rather live near their white friends in Montana.

It wasn't until 1910 that by an act of Congress the wandering tribes received the joyous and long-sought-after news that they were to be given part of the old Fort Assinniboine Military Reservation as their permanent home.

Only Rocky Boy, the beloved chief of the Ojibwa Chippewa, wasn't there, for he had died a short time before. Nevertheless, in honor of their great chief, the new land they were given was called Rocky Boy Reservation.

Somewhere above them on the Hanging Road, *ekutsihimmiyo*, all of the Ojibwa Chippewa knew their beloved chief would, as he walked along this path for the souls of the dead on their journey to the afterlife, be aware of the good fortune that had at last come to his people.

And many rejoiced, for themselves, and for Rocky Boy.

POWELL'S ARMY
BY TERENCE DUNCAN

#1: UNCHAINED LIGHTNING   (1994, $2.50)
Thundering out of the past, a trio of deadly enforcers dispenses its own brand of frontier justice throughout the untamed American West! Two men and one woman, they are the U.S. Army's most lethal secret weapon—they are POWELL'S ARMY!

#2: APACHE RAIDERS   (2073, $2.50)
The disappearance of seventeen Apache maidens brings tribal unrest to the violent breaking point. To prevent an explosion of bloodshed, Powell's Army races through a nightmare world south of the border—and into the deadly clutches of a vicious band of Mexican flesh merchants!

#3: MUSTANG WARRIORS   (2171, $2.50)
Someone is selling cavalry guns and horses to the Comanche—and that spells trouble for the bluecoats' campaign against Chief Quanah Parker's bloodthirsty Kwahadi warriors. But Powell's Army are no strangers to trouble. When the showdown comes, they'll be ready—and someone is going to die!

#4: ROBBERS ROOST   (2285, $2.50)
After hijacking an army payroll wagon and killing the troopers riding guard, Three-Fingered Jack and his gang high-tail it into Virginia City to spend their ill-gotten gains. But Powell's Army plans to apprehend the murderous hardcases before the local vigilantes do—to make sure that Jack and his slimy band stretch hemp the legal way!

THRILLERS BY WILLIAM W. JOHNSTONE

THE DEVIL'S CAT (2091, $3.95)

The town was alive with all kinds of cats. Black, white, fat, scrawny. They lived in the streets, in backyards, in the swamps of Becancour. Sam, Nydia, and Little Sam had never seen so many cats. The cats' eyes were glowing slits as they watched the newcomers. The town was ripe with evil. It seemed to waft in from the swamps with the hot, fetid breeze and breed in the minds of Becancour's citizens. Soon Sam, Nydia, and Little Sam would battle the forces of darkness. Standing alone against the ultimate predator—The Devil's Cat.

THE DEVIL'S HEART (2110, $3.95)

Now it was summer again in Whitfield. The town was peaceful, quiet, and unprepared for the atrocities to come. Eternal life, everlasting youth, an orgy that would span time—that was what the Lord of Darkness was promising the coven members in return for their pledge of love. The few who had fought against his hideous powers before, believed it could never happen again. Then the hot wind began to blow—as black as evil as The Devil's Heart.

THE DEVIL'S TOUCH (2111, $3.95)

Once the carnage begins, there's no time for anything but terror. Hollow-eyed, hungry corpses rise from unearthly tombs to gorge themselves on living flesh and spawn a new generation of restless Undead. The demons of Hell cavort with Satan's unholy disciples in blood-soaked rituals and fevered orgies. The Balons have faced the red, glowing eyes of the Master before, and they know what must be done. But there can be no salvation for those marked by The Devil's Touch.

Available wherever paperbacks are sold, or order direct from the Publisher. Send cover price plus 50¢ per copy for mailing and handling to Zebra Books, Dept. 2920, 475 Park Avenue South, New York, N.Y. 10016. Residents of New York, New Jersey and Pennsylvania must include sales tax. DO NOT SEND CASH.